THE CHRISTMAS
HUMMINGBIRD

Center Point
Large Print

Also by Davis Bunn and available from
Center Point Large Print:

Firefly Cove
Moondust Lake
Outbreak
Unscripted
Tranquility Falls
Burden of Proof
The Emerald Tide
The Cottage on Lighthouse Lane

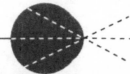

**This Large Print Book carries the
Seal of Approval of N.A.V.H.**

THE CHRISTMAS HUMMINGBIRD

DAVIS BUNN

CENTER POINT LARGE PRINT
THORNDIKE, MAINE

This Center Point Large Print edition
is published in the year 2022 by arrangement with
Kensington Publishing Corp.

The text of this Large Print edition is unabridged.
In other aspects, this book may vary
from the original edition.
Printed in the United States of America
on permanent paper sourced using
environmentally responsible foresting methods.
Set in 16-point Times New Roman type.

ISBN: 978-1-63808-570-6

The Library of Congress has cataloged this record
under Library of Congress Control Number: 2022944265

This book is dedicated to:

TONY COLLINS

Steadfast guide
Lifelong friend

PROLOGUE

Three and a half weeks before Christmas, Ethan Lange woke to a pounding on his door. Hammering with something other than fists, a solid metallic banging punctuated by shouts.

He had been so deeply asleep it felt as though he carried his slumber with him. When he opened his door, two sweating and ash-streaked faces yelled at him that the canyon fire had shifted, the wind was rising, and Ethan had three minutes to gather his belongings and flee.

All his questions and protests died unspoken as a shift in the wind sent live cinders cascading over his front yard and the police car and the fire truck. He gaped in confused panic as the sky rained burning flakes over his world.

The policewoman gripped his arm and yelled, "Sir, do you hear me? Now means *now!*"

Then had come a sound Ethan would never forget, a soft explosive *whoom*. Ethan was pushed back a step by the force. It punched his chest like a nightmare fist.

The two sweating faces and their hi-viz jackets shone a brilliant yellow in his workshop's exploding butane tanks. They both staggered and almost went down.

The firefighter grabbed the shoulder of Ethan's T-shirt and dragged him out of the house and over to the police car. He opened the passenger door, tossed Ethan inside, and yelled to the policewoman, "We got the last house! *Go! Go!*"

The woman spoke a few words as she started off. Shouted, actually. But all Ethan could hear was the pounding of his own heart.

She drove with an expert's tight calm, racing the walls of fire that now consumed both sides of his beloved canyon. They sped past three huge bonfires, all that was left of his neighbors and closest friends. He started to ask if they got out, then stopped. To hear any bad news just then would have been more than he could bear.

A few minutes or hours later—Ethan had no sense of time's passage, none whatsoever—the policewoman did a four-wheel spin at the boundary of a collection point. She pointed at the yellow school bus. "That's your ticket out."

Ethan saw a collection of frightened faces in most of the school bus windows, illuminated by the flickering light. "What about you?"

"One last canyon, then I'm done." When Ethan did not move, she said, "You need—"

"Thank you. So much."

She looked at him then, and to Ethan, it seemed as though she really saw him for the first time. She said softly, "You need to go now."

He rose from the vehicle and stood there in his

underwear and T-shirt and bare feet as she spun away. Hands gripped him and gently led him toward the bus. Other hands draped a blanket over his shoulders. As he climbed the stairs and settled into an empty seat, Ethan thought it was incredibly strange, almost ridiculous, that all he could think of at that moment was the woman who had saved him. Streaked face, bulky jacket, copper-dark gaze, voice made for softly issuing commands.

Beautiful.

1

Twelve days before Christmas, Ethan Lange woke to the smell of ashes and the hum of tiny wings.

He'd had the same predawn dream every night since losing his home. It stayed with him as he padded into the kitchen and made coffee. Six months earlier, Ethan had been wandering around the streets behind Miramar's business district and came upon a nearly derelict home with a FOR SALE BY OWNER sign planted in the front weeds. The house was scarcely nine hundred square feet, an abused vacation home on an oversized yard. The asking price basically covered the cost of land, with a few thousand extra for the building permits already in place. Ethan had no idea why he had bought it. His life was already overfull. He had a second job that brought in a good, if unsteady, income. But instead of flipping the property, as he probably should have, he slowly launched himself into the renovation process and found he loved it.

Once work on the roof and electricity and plumbing and windows was completed, Ethan tore out the kitchen. Then the bathroom. He spent the next two weekends stripping away the rotting carpets and replacing almost a quarter of the floorboards. He then decided the ceiling needed to go as well. Out went the awful drop-down squares, in came a crew to help tear out the insulation, sand and polish the rafters, and set in place a new A-frame ceiling of polished maple.

Ethan ate breakfast standing by the new counter, surveying his open-plan main room. The house still contained the vague smell of paint and sawdust. His kitchen held a few plates, two cheap pots, a meager collection of utensils. All his clothes, except two new business suits, were gifts from neighbors and colleagues. His fridge was full to bursting with food, his cupboards crammed with booze and wine. Almost everybody who dropped off gifts calmly ignored his thanks.

He found an odd sense of comfort being sheltered in a home he had rebuilt. It did not fill the empty spaces caused by the fire. But it helped. A lot.

Breakfast done, he sorted through the three shipping crates seeing duty as his closet, came up with a clean shirt and trousers and tie, and headed out.

He walked the seven blocks to work beneath a china-blue sky. Mid-December usually saw the early winter storms come sweeping in from the Pacific, windswept furies that lashed the town with much-needed rain. But this year, the desert winds continued to push in from the east, months after they normally faded into memory. They gave rise to the driest autumn anyone could remember, following upon the hottest summer on record.

It had rained once in September, a squall that lashed the coast for a day and a half. The locals took it as a good sign, for such winter storms were vital. They filled the reservoirs and eased the threat of fires wreaking havoc through the inland valleys. Only this year, the squall passed, the skies cleared, and the desert winds returned. Blowing acrid and constant right through October and into November. By Thanksgiving, Ethan's morning drives into work were marked by people standing in clusters, up and down Miramar's main streets. All of their faces turned east, searching, fretting.

A week later, smoke began staining the cloudless sky.

Nowadays even the softest morning breeze carried a hint of smoke. By midafternoon, the smell of distant fires dominated the town.

Ethan considered California Christmases to be rainbow events—as in, explosive colors fashioned from the locals' various heritages. Miramar had a strong Latino population, mostly Mexican, but a considerable number of Ecuadorians and Colombians. They were never more passionate about their traditions than at Christmas, which made the town very lively indeed: There were parties and fiestas. Music and lights and fireworks. Singing and laughter and too much food. Even this year, when wildfires streaked the sky with dark ribbons and everyone worried about the future of their town.

For the past six years, Christmas had been little more than a time of marking the anniversary of his divorce and the end of his marriage. He had found it almost natural to retreat from the town and its festive air. He did not resent others celebrating. He simply felt excluded.

Central Coast Savings and Loan occupied the largest building on Miramar's main business street. It was also the town's oldest bank, founded in the early days of the twentieth century and still possessing the stolid grace of earlier times. Ethan arrived at precisely ten minutes to nine and stared at his reflection in the glass doors, a tall and slim and precise man in his mid-thirties. Finally Dolores, the head teller, unlocked the doors and ushered him inside.

The bank was decorated with a small tree and three holly wreaths and a long stream of ivy above the teller windows, all holding lights that blinked a cheery welcome. The bank's main chamber was huge, with a granite-tiled floor and a mahogany central standing-desk. The ceiling was twenty-four feet high, with lovely Spanish-style painted rafters and a trio of brass chandeliers. Ethan's desk was situated behind a waist-high barrier of carved redwood, with a little swinging door as his entry.

The day proceeded along its holiday season course. Slow and cheery, with a pause at lunch-time for a miniature office party. Ethan pretended to drink a cup of mildly spiked eggnog and enjoyed the gentle pranks of exchanging mystery gifts with people whose names were drawn from a hat. What was not to love.

As the afternoon wound down, a call came in on his direct line. His closest friend in Los Angeles greeted him: "I know you said never to call your office. But I've been trying to reach you for a week."

"I lost my phone in the fire."

"If that's a joke, it's a bad one."

Ethan had been working on and off for Noah Hearst since the year after his divorce. What had once been a secret passion had gradually become a second profession. Ethan enjoyed working with Noah, even under the high-pressure conditions that dominated everything to do with the world of Hollywood. "No joke. The fire swept down my valley in less than half an hour. All I took out was the T-shirt and jockey shorts I was wearing. Not even a pair of shoes."

Noah said, "I'm so sorry."

"Life goes on," Ethan replied. He gave Noah the number to his new cell.

"I'd be happy to offer you space in my operation."

"You mean, move to LA?"

"Just for a few months."

"Not even for a few minutes."

"Put a little more venom in that response. Tell me what you really think of my town."

"Is there anything else I can do for you? A mortgage on a vacation home?"

"I need your help with a new project. Harvey Chambers, head of Chambers Broadcasting, heard of him?"

"The name, sure."

"He wants to resurrect a Christmas story that's been out of print for decades. He was raised on them. They're seven books in all, and Harvey thinks they'll be a hit with a new generation."

"Seven books, you said."

"Right."

Ethan felt a kindling of unaccustomed excitement. "Not the Elven Child."

Noah went quiet. Then, "Okay, this is spooky."

"The Elven Child books were my absolute favorite stories as a kid. My grandparents had a full set. I read them until they fell apart."

"Wow."

"What?"

"Those were almost Harvey's exact words. Apparently, he was orphaned at an early age. Raised by his grandparents. His grandfather introduced Harvey to the books. It formed a bond that got him through some very tough times."

"I like the man already."

"So do I, and I was with the guy for exactly ninety seconds. Less. Their in-house producer thinks the world of Chambers." Noah paused. "There's a kicker."

"There usually is."

"CBC is notoriously tight when it comes to production budgets. The executive board sees this whole project as a huge risk. Chambers has ordered them to resurrect a series that hasn't been in print for almost fifty years. They're talking a minuscule budget."

"I'd do this work for free."

"For the record, that's not the smartest negotiating tactic I've ever heard."

"I mean it. Count me in."

"They're tentatively planning the first film for next year's Christmas special. Wait, I've got the name down here somewhere."

"*The Crystal Pipe.*"

"Which means we've got to jump on this." Noah's words accelerated. "They want this as a mix of live action and CGI. Did you ever see the film *Beetlejuice?*"

"Years ago."

"Shot in the late eighties, won an Academy Award, big hit. It uses a miniature village for part of the action, supposedly shrinking down

16

the characters for those scenes. Chambers wants us to use a similar setup to introduce the elves. Apparently he plans on staying personally involved. Which may be good and may be an awful waste of time." Noah waited. "Hello?"

"Thinking."

"According to Harvey, the idea is to shoot several scenes when they pan over this model village. Credits, dream sequences, the first time the child sees the elves. They do live in a village, correct?"

"Yes, Noah. Inside a tree."

A silence, then: "How do they get a town inside a tree? Do elves shrink in this story?"

"That's part of the magic. Have you even read the stories?"

"I've got orders out with two rare-book stores. The producer's promised me a script as soon as it gets in-house approval. Back to the subject at hand."

"A miniature elven village, built on a miniature budget. Got it."

"I'll pay you what I can," Noah promised. "If it's a hit, we've been offered a seven-film deal. And a bigger budget moving forward. So, when can I expect your initial designs?"

2

Ryan entered the party wondering if she would ever get the smell of smoke out of her hair. The crowd was good natured and well-oiled and getting both noisy and loose. She saw a couple of younger men shift their attention to her, and wondered if there was going to be trouble. But before they could make a move, their boss waved and started over.

"Ryan Eames, did I get that right?"

"Thanks for inviting me, Mr. Acosta."

"Please, I'm Berto to my pals." He was big and ruddy and strong in a manner that belied his fifty-something age. "Any officer working with Porter Wright is a friend in my book. Can I get you a drink?"

"Thanks, but I'm on duty."

He surveyed her outfit, a Versace pantsuit she had found on the designer rack at Off Fifth. "Miramar's police ladies are definitely going up market." He gestured with the hand holding his drink at the mostly male crowd watching them. "There's about sixty dozen of my buddies out there who are waiting for the chance to make your acquaintance. A few of them might even be single. And a lot more who wish they were."

"Do us both a favor, and tell them my badge is

in my purse. Along with my faithful companion, Mister Glock."

He had a big laugh, open and happy. "I like you, Ryan. Okay if I call you that?"

"It's my name."

He pointed them across the room. "Why don't we take this over to where my wife can see I'm not trying out any rusty moves of my own. She's the lovely lady watching us like a hawk."

Berto Acosta owned one of the central coast's largest home builders. His annual Christmas party filled Miramar's town hall and spilled onto both front and rear porches. A band was setting up on the chamber's stubby stage, while a dozen bow-tied waiters hovered around the bar and buffet line. Ryan asked, "What can you tell me about Ethan Lange?"

Berto lost his smile. "Who wants to know—the cop or this nice-looking lady?"

"I told you, sir. I'm on the job."

Berto did not speak again until they stood before his wife. "Hon, this is Ryan Eames. Ryan, Amelia. Officer Eames is interested in Ethan."

The woman's gaze was dark, glacial. "Why are you asking about my friend?"

Ryan took note of the woman's protective anger, decided it actually worked in her favor. "It's a highly sensitive matter."

She shook her head. "Uh-uh, lady. That doesn't work in my book. Not with Ethan."

"He's not in any kind of trouble, if that's what concerns you. I have a very special assignment. I need his help."

Her husband offered, "Porter vouches for her."

Amelia continued to burn Ryan with her gaze. "So tell us about this assignment."

Ryan heard the woman's challenge. Loud and clear. "It's best if you didn't discuss this with others."

"Do I look like I want to gossip? Me, refusing to talk about Ethan until you clarify just exactly what it is that you're wanting from my friend?"

Ryan decided she liked this woman. "About half of the homes under threat from the fire are currently vacant."

"Sure. Second homes used for weekends and vacations," Berto said. "They're some of my best customers."

"We need to check out homes after they've been caught in the fire line," Ryan said. "Some of the structures remain partially intact. Others have safes or fireproof cellars. I'm hoping I can convince Mr. Lange to help secure items that haven't been destroyed—"

"Ethan's perfect," Berto declared.

"He's a good and honest man," his wife agreed.

Ryan looked from one to the other, saw a pair of confident expressions. She found herself wondering if her own friends would be so, well, definite. "Can you give me a little more to go on?"

Amelia said, "We have an expression, '*Tiene muchos trasfondos.*' "

"Many hidden depths," Berto translated. "That's our Ethan."

"You think he is a banker. And he is. A good one."

"The best," Berto said. "He handles the finance for all my construction projects."

"He is also a good man. With a very good heart. A wounded heart, but good just the same."

"He still carries a flame for his ex-wife," Berto said. "He's been divorced, what, five years now?"

"Six years this week," Amelia corrected. "And the lady police officer does not need to know any more of Ethan's personal details."

"Actually," Ryan said, "anything like this can help."

"You want personal? Fine." To her husband: "Show her the picture."

Berto already had his phone out and was scrolling. He passed over his phone. "This is Ethan's work."

"More than work," Amelia said. "His secret life."

"Not so much secret as, what's the word I'm looking for." To Ryan, "Ethan doesn't hide it away. He just doesn't talk about it. To anyone. Ever."

"Secret works just fine," Amelia replied. "We may be the only people in Miramar who know of this. His ex-wife, she probably knew and forgot. That woman. Hmph. He is better off without her."

"Amelia."

"Well, it's true."

Ryan stared at a palace jutting into a night sky. The central turret almost touched a crescent moon. "I don't understand. Ethan Lange built this?"

"What you see, it's a model." Amelia shaped the air in front of her. "This big."

Berto said, "We had a daughter. She died seven years ago."

"Almost eight," Amelia corrected. "My husband and dates. Impossible."

"I'm so sorry."

"She was six," Berto said. "Leukemia."

"My angel was crazy for princess stories and princess dolls." Amelia pointed to Berto's phone. "Ethan built this for her last Christmas on this earth."

"He never would take payment," Berto said. "Or let us give him back the model."

"How could he take our money. It was a gift. To our angel. And you were wrong to offer." To Ryan, "We gave the model and all her dolls to the Catholic orphanage. They became prizes in their Christmas raffle. Raised almost five thousand dollars."

"Ethan's dollhouses are sold years out," Berto said.

"The man is an artist with miniatures."

"He does a lot of work for some Hollywood set designer. Models and something like cartoons, I forget the word."

"Claymation. His work has been on any number of children's films and TV programs." Amelia nodded. "An artist, our Ethan."

"Our little girl, she was just over the moon." Berto smiled sadly at the memory. "She played with it right to the end. Then we moved in a table so she could look at it, you know, whenever."

Amelia demanded, "What else do you want to know?"

Ryan scarcely recognized her own voice. "I have all I need, thank you."

Berto glanced at the doorway. "Here he comes now."

Ryan did not follow Berto toward the main entrance. Instead, she stepped to the bar and accepted a glass of California champagne. But she did not drink. She simply needed a moment to digest what she had just witnessed.

She had seen the openhearted concern and affection in both their gazes. Amelia, Berto's wife, had shown the ferociousness of a mother cat protecting one of her own. And the palace, what a work of art! All this from a man she had assumed was just a banker. Someone she could possibly use during the current crisis.

Instead, she watched as one person after another approached Ethan Lange and shook his hand, shouted a welcome, gestured with their glass, saying clear as day that the man was not just welcome, but an essential element to the night's festivities. Berto actually embraced him before turning and pointing in Ryan's direction.

On the surface, Ethan was just like his photograph. He was perhaps a trace over six feet, mild in expression, giving little away. He was trim, with brown hair cut short, dressed in khakis and a blue button-down shirt, both probably brand new. His calm green eyes studied her over the surrounding people. Ryan had the impression that the loss of his home had left him bruised, but far from bowed.

She forced herself to set down the glass and start forward. There was no reason the man should frighten her so. None at all.

3

Berto's Christmas party was pretty much as Ethan expected. Three times the number of men as women. Big hands, loud voices, solid bodies, more than a few becoming nasty and aggressive as they downed too many drinks. Theirs was a tough line of work, pushing hard against the clock and the calendar, a hundred different risks and a thousand reasons for a project to go wrong.

Ethan handled all the bank's mortgages and most of the construction loans. Some of the region's best builders were brawlers by nature. Just like his father had been. Ethan knew some looked down on him, the money guy, the geek who never got his hands dirty, the soft-spoken numbers wimp. Some assumed he was gay, including a few of those who knew he'd been married for two and a half years. Ethan occasionally wondered if his wife was behind that rumor. He minded. Some, not a lot. He'd been paying the price for his quiet and modest manner since childhood.

Berto Acosta, the company president, shook his hand and reached over for a man-size embrace at the same time, spilling bourbon on his shoulder. "How come you don't have a drink, boyo?"

"I haven't even had time to find the bar yet." Ethan surveyed the city hall, the Christmas lights, the band playing eighties hits, the crowd pushing their way around the buffet line. "Great party."

"We tried to book the Castaways restaurant. But the boss lady said, not ever again."

Ethan gave that the smile it deserved. Six Christmases ago, Berto had celebrated his best-ever year with a party at Miramar's premier restaurant. Toward daybreak, a couple of the bricklayers had done their best to remodel the back room. The kitchen staff had shown the fierce loyalty of professional bouncers and tossed the entire crowd into the street.

Ethan had left hours before all that happened. Hand in hand with his soon-to-be former wife. It was the last event they had ever attended together. Other than divorce court.

The nervous flicker in Berto's gaze showed the big man had just thought of the very same thing. He took a heavy swig from his glass, then used it to point toward the bar. "There's a pretty lady, been asking about you."

Ethan was astonished he had not noticed her before. She stood in an island all her very own, a dozen or so men watching her every move, none of them willing to pierce the invisible veil.

"What's Officer Eames doing here?"

"Wanting to talk with you, apparently. You know her?"

"We've met. Sort of." Ethan started over. "She saved my life."

Crossing the room gave Ethan ample time to form a second impression. Much of it was in line with his first. Of course her dress was different. The bulky hi-viz yellow jacket was absent. The sweat and ash that had streaked her features, the hair matted to her head when she dumped her helmet on the rear seat, all gone. But the tensile strength was the same, slender and taut as a rapier's blade. Ethan saw how most of the other men shot glances her way, or gazed at her openly. But no one approached. She was certainly attractive, but her hard-edged features were coupled with a direct, no-nonsense gaze. Ryan Eames looked and breathed her profession.

Ethan guessed her age at early thirties, but could have been off by five years, maybe more. She held herself very erect, very aware. Like a bird of prey waiting for the reason to launch herself into flight.

Ethan stepped up beside her, greeted the bartender, and asked Ryan, "What are you drinking?"

"I asked for a glass of champagne. I have no idea why. I'm on duty." She told the bartender, "Can I have a Coke?"

"Coming right up. Ethan?"

"Same, Jeff. Thanks."

She asked, "You know everyone here?"

"Most of them. It's a small town. Three banks.

Ours is the largest." He nodded his thanks to the bartender, took a sip, said, "Berto said you've been asking about me."

"That's right. I have."

"If you wanted to know something, why didn't you come to me directly?"

"It's a sensitive issue."

Ethan liked that about her. The direct answer. No hiding or avoiding. "Did you learn what you needed about me?"

"I think so. Yes."

He took his time, studying her. She would tell him when she was ready. Or not. This was not a lady who could be pressed into doing anything against her will. A few moments in her company, mostly speeding down fire-rimmed roads, was enough to know she was very much her own woman. "I came by the station to thank you."

"Porter told me. I think that was why he suggested we meet." She picked up her glass, set it down again. "You're the only one who's lost everything, then came around to thank us."

"The only reason we're having this conversation is because you got there in time."

"Me and the fellows on the front line."

"I thanked them too." Ethan suspected she merely tolerated the way he stared. She was not as tall as he remembered. As if the panic and the night and racing against the firestorm had altered his memory of her. All her features, every inch of her frame, were honed down to their very essence. And something else. *Vigilant* was a word that had long gone out of fashion. Ryan Eames held to a taut readiness. The woman waited for the next reason to spring into flight. Toward the next danger.

She asked, "Join me outside?"

"Sure thing." He followed her through the party. If she was bothered by how most of the male eyes tracked her progress, or even if she noticed, Ryan gave no sign. The broad porch was as crowded as inside, so she continued on down the stairs and into the street.

A voice called as he passed, "Everything okay there, Ethan?"

"Just fine."

"She gets out the handcuffs, you be sure and give me a call."

Ethan waved to someone he could not be bothered to identify. The streetlight overhead was out, and the shadows cast her features into a craven image. "What can I do for you?"

"The county sheriffs are overstretched. I've been seconded to assist with patrolling the local valleys, which is how you and I met. You've probably heard the forecast is not good."

"Yes." It was the primary topic of conversation. Another blow out of the east, expected gusts topping fifty miles per hour. "The last thing we need."

"I'm tasked with checking out homes that have been caught by the fire."

Ethan felt a wave of queasiness. "You look for bodies?"

"No. First responders in the fire team have that duty." She held to the same flat tone. Weather, bodies, no change. "You know the Crescent Valley?"

"Of course." Some of Miramar's most luxurious estates lined the Crescent Ridge. Though most of the homes were cash purchases, Ethan carried a couple of those mortgages. The amounts were staggering.

"One segment of the blaze has reached the next valley over. Only thirty percent contained."

Ethan nodded. He had heard that too.

"If the wind comes up like they predict, the Crescent homes will be evacuated. Nineteen in all. Fire chiefs think there's every chance some of the houses will go. Maybe all of them."

"That's terrible."

"There's more. Very confidential. We can't have this getting out."

"My word on it."

"We suspect the fire might have been deliberately started."

"What?"

"Nothing's certain. But the way it's spread, the homes now in its path, there is a chance." It was her turn to study him. Moving in close enough, he caught a hint of her perfume. And something else. A chemical odor, fire retardant perhaps. Ethan shivered, as if the flames had suddenly entered the town itself. She went on, "First responders have spotted what we think is a crew working the wreckage."

"I don't . . . Crew?"

"Robbers. Very professional. Fast in and out. Dressed in the same gear as the fire crews, but when they were hailed, they scattered."

Ethan clenched down on a sudden burst of rage.

Despite the darkness, Ryan noticed the change. "You okay?"

"Yes, it's just . . . The thought of other families enduring what I've gone through because of robbers . . ."

She nodded slowly. As if she approved. "Our force here in Miramar is very small."

"I know. Seven officers."

"I've talked it over with Porter. He agrees. We'd like to deputize you." Her words accelerated, as if she needed to get it all out before he refused. "Soon as the fire crews give us the all-clear, we move. Day or night. Our aim is to gather valuables that escape the blaze. We want to—"

"I accept."

"There's an element of risk involved. You need to understand—"

"The only reason I'm alive is because you

got there ahead of the flames. I want to do this. Please."

Her teeth gleamed in the streetlight. "I thought it would be a lot harder than this."

He returned her smile. "When do we start?"

4

Eight fifteen the next morning, Ethan was standing in the police station's front room when Porter Wright, Miramar's police chief, arrived for duty. Ethan's swearing-in took sixty seconds. Less. Porter recited the words in a rush, buckling his heavy belt and filling it with his equipment as he did so. A robbery had been called in, pushing the station into overdrive.

Porter thanked him, then opened the top right drawer and passed over a badge. "Carry this with you whenever you're on a call. You suffer from asthma or any other issue with your breathing?"

"No, none."

Porter slid a thick pamphlet across his desk. "Fire safety instructions. Probably won't be necessary, since you're coming in after the crews give the all-clear. But you need to study it just the same."

"Do I get a gun?"

"Can you shoot?"

"A little. Not well."

"Then no. Absolutely not. I won't be party to my newest deputy injuring himself or some innocent third party." He grabbed his hat and

33

rushed out, calling over his shoulder as he departed, "Welcome aboard."

Ethan was late getting to the bank, such a rarity that a number of the other employees stopped by to ask if he was okay. When he explained his new volunteer role, Ethan was surprised at how enthusiastic the others became. Carl Reese, the bank's president, confessed, "I've started to put my name in the hat a dozen times. More. But the idea of running toward those flames . . ."

"Scares me silly," senior teller Dolores agreed.

Ethan asked, "You're okay with my doing this?"

"Absolutely."

"I have no idea when I might be called out. I'll make up the hours best I can."

"Don't worry about it. Six business days until we break for Christmas, what urgent action could you possibly miss?"

"You're doing this for all of us scaredy-cats." Dolores was a heavyset woman who showed a motherly affection to everyone she liked. She added, "Just don't you dare get hurt."

By midafternoon, it seemed the whole town knew. Customers stopped by his desk, thanked him for what he was doing. A few found quiet humor in calling him "Deputy." When he mentioned it to Carl around closing, it was Dolores who replied. "Look around here. What do you see? Frightened people who wish they could do more for all those fire victims."

"Everybody in Miramar knows someone who's lost everything," Carl agreed.

"Not to mention how worried everyone is over the fire making it to town," Dolores added.

"Don't say it," Carl told her. "Don't even think it."

"We're all involved, whether we like it or not," Dolores went on. "Churches, clubs, you name it."

"The fires define the season," Carl said.

"Everybody knows you've been hurt by this. Now look at you. Trying to help out others who've been through the same." She hugged him, a first. "Christmas for some folks will only happen because of people like you."

The words kept him warm company through a solitary dinner. There was little of interest on television, and the book he had found fascinating the previous night was so tedious he finally gave up and went to bed.

It seemed like only an instant, hardly more than a few heartbeats of slumber, before the phone woke him. But the clock on the screen read twenty-seven minutes past midnight.

"Hello?"

"It's Ryan." She sounded as calm as ever. "I'm parked outside. We're on."

5

They had scarcely made it past the Miramar city-limits sign, decked out with fairy lights and a smiling Santa, when the night was riven by a long streamer of flames. Ryan assured him the burning ridgeline was over ten miles away. Which meant the flames he saw had to be fifty feet high, maybe twice that.

They got held up at the firebreak station, a massive confusion of trucks and people and equipment and smoke. Ryan left the engine running and told Ethan to remain in the vehicle while she spoke to the assistant chief. The woman was already walking towards them, there to greet Ryan as she rose from the car. Ethan thought both their faces held a tight adrenaline gleam.

Ryan returned to the car, slipped behind the wheel, and sat tapping her fingers on the wheel. "Too slow. Too slow."

Ethan found it hard to take in the controlled chaos beyond their silent vehicle. Finally a dirt-streaked ER wagon rolled up, and a sweaty face appeared in the window long enough to cough and wave for them to follow.

Progress meant weaving around falling branches,

then they halted altogether when a sudden gust blew fiery cinders across the road ahead. The drive seemed endless, but probably took less than twenty minutes.

Their destination was a former ranch, converted into a luxury getaway, and now turned to rubble. Ethan thought he was going to be physically sick when he rose from the police car and surveyed the wreckage. Everything he had lost. All the small elements that had once made up his life. Gone.

Ryan watched him as she opened her trunk and donned the fire-retardant gear. "You okay?"

"Yes. It's just . . ."

"Hard. I know." She fitted the mask around her face. "Hold tight. I'll be back quick as I can."

Ten minutes later, she returned, pulled off the mask, wiped her face, and tossed the bottle into the trunk. "There's something you need to see." She pulled a second yellow slicker from the trunk. "In the future, you need to wear clothes and boots that are only for this duty. They'll get ruined in the process. Sorry, I should have mentioned this earlier."

Ethan slipped on the jacket and decided there was no need to remind her of how limited his wardrobe had become. "No problem."

As they approached the house, Ryan said, "We won't need a breathing unit. We're not going inside the home." She called to the ER driver standing by his door. "Shine the light over there, Horace."

"You got it." He swung the side lamp around, momentarily blinding Ethan.

When he could see, he found Ryan pointing to a pair of lines dug deep into what had previously been the home's front lawn. "Are those—"

"Tire tracks. Deep ones." Ryan reached out her hand, and the ER driver had a camera ready. She began shooting pictures and continued. "Big truck tires, looks like a double rear-axle." She walked forward a half-dozen paces. "See this?"

"Yes." It was hard to miss. An even wider divot was carved between the tire tracks, leading up to where Ryan stood. It looked like the truck had plowed a knee-deep furrow in the muddy ash.

"They used a wrecker to pull a safe from the wall." She pointed to the home's skeletal remains and called, "Horace?"

"On it."

The light swung up, revealing the remnants of an interior supporting wall of massive stone blocks. One central section gaped open like a missing tooth. Ryan went on, "They dragged it out here, lifted it onto the truck bed, and off they went." She turned to Horace. "You'll pass this on to Maya?"

"Loud and clear, Officer Lady."

"Ask her to speak with the fire chief. We need to be out here with the first responders."

Horace shook his head. "You know as well as I do, Maya can talk herself blue in the face, but the chief won't budge on that."

"I guess I'll have to do it myself."

"Same answer."

Ryan pressed, "We need to be surveying these properties soon as the fire clears. Before, if he'll let us." Ryan started back to the car. "Come on, Ethan. Our work here is done."

Ryan followed the EMS truck back to the ready station, where Ethan watched her argue with the fire chief, scrolling through the photos on their camera. Maya Ricardo, the assistant chief, added her voice to Ryan's. But it didn't help. Ethan could see the fire chief was adamant. Ryan returned to her vehicle with a full head of steam.

They were almost back to town before she spoke. "The chief and most of the crews consider our work as just another item far down a long list. They see their primary jobs as killing the fire and keeping their crews safe. Everything else is just flotsam."

Ethan had not spoken a word since leaving the site. The whole experience was simply overwhelming. "Do you ever have nightmares?"

"Not that I recall. I almost never remember my dreams." She stayed silent so long, Ethan suspected that was all he was going to get. Then she added, "Sometimes I wake up sweating.

Heart pounding. But I don't know why. Those nights can get very long."

Ethan nodded. "Ever since the fire, I wake up smelling smoke and . . ."

"What?"

"It sounds crazy, even in my head."

She flashed her lights at the smiling Santa and reentered Miramar proper. "That's what cops on patrol duty do. They let out the crazy."

"Why did you do that? Flash your lights at the sign."

"I don't know. Habit. Every time I make it back in one piece, I feel like it's nice to tell the town hello. If I'm by myself, I wish Santa a merry Christmas."

"Out loud?"

She nodded. "I know. Crazy, right?"

Ethan rolled down his window, stuck out his head, and shouted out behind them, *"Merry Christmas, Santa!"*

Ryan watched him roll up the window. They shared a smile. But as they entered Miramar, Ethan had the distinct impression that her features took on a sorrowful cast.

Then she said, "I have a son." Her words were softly spoken and carried a weight. "He's eleven. And I'm worried sick."

Ethan responded by pulling the seat belt far enough away from his chest to swing around and face her.

40

"Liam is a fine, sweet, caring boy. And smart, it's amazing to watch him. But his health, it's . . ."

"Delicate?"

"Basically since birth. First it was one thing, then another, three times in the hospital before his second birthday. The past few years, he's stayed healthy. But every time a neighbor catches a bug, I hold my breath."

Ethan sat there. Watching. Content to wait as long as she needed.

"I hate the word *fragile*. *Delicate* I can handle most of the time. Not always. He's such a strong boy in so many ways."

"What does he like?"

"That's the problem. The crisis in a nutshell. All Liam does is draw. All he wants to do. His teachers think he's slow. He thinks *they're* slow. Or just not of any interest." A soft burr entered her voice. "The other kids make fun of him. He's, I don't know . . ."

"Defenseless."

"How do you know?"

Ethan shook his head. "Another time. What about television? Games?"

"He watches cartoons. He asks for computer games, plays them for, I don't know, a few days. Never very long. Then he stops and he draws what he sees. Or what he thinks they should have done."

"It's not the game. It's the art."

"Same question again. How do you know this?"

"If I was his age, I'd probably be the same way."

"Berto told me about your models. Working for the Hollywood producer." She attempted a smile. "That must be exciting."

He started to correct her, explain how he worked for the set designer, who, in turn, was hired by producers. But he didn't want the conversation to get sidetracked. "I'd love to see his work."

"So would I." The quietly spoken sadness returned. "Liam is so secretive. I'll sneak in sometimes when he's in school, look through his drawings. They're amazing. But I'm his mom, which means I'm terribly biased. Plus I don't know a thing about art."

Ethan waited, but she did not offer anything else. He had no idea how to respond, but did not want the night to end on such an uneven note. When she pulled up in front of his home, he said the only thing that came to mind. "I dream I hear hummingbird wings."

"You mean, when you smell . . ."

"The ashes. Right. I used to have hummingbird feeders all around my home. Both porches, lining the path to my workshop, four on the garage's corners. After my divorce, it felt good having the company. They just became part of my life." In the quiet that followed, he could almost hear the hum of those feathered beasts. "I miss them. I miss my home."

She studied him a long moment, then said, "Have dinner with me. With us. Tomorrow."

6

That night, for the first time in ages, Ryan dreamed and remembered it upon awakening.

It was not a nightmare, not by any stretch of the imagination. Why Ryan woke up gasping for breath, her heart hammering, she had no idea.

In her dream, the wildfire had passed. She was driving on a canyon road, following a fire truck and an ERT vehicle. Their flashing lights were almost blanketed by dust and ash. She drove past the long line of vehicles waiting to be allowed back to what once had been their homes. Entering the burn area, everything gone, the homes and trees and brush, everything. Half a mile was enough for her car to be covered with ashes. Using the windshield wipers to clear the glass, Ryan slowed as she passed the former home of friends, nothing but the blackened chimney remaining.

Then she looked up and realized she was alone.

The two lead vehicles had vanished. The road ahead was utterly empty. Ryan stepped on the gas and sped around a curve . . .

And there he was.

Her son stood in the middle of the road. Liam was dressed all in white. He was utterly untouched by the surrounding ashes. A flash of purity amidst all the blackened memories. He stared at her with a solemn gaze.

She stopped the car and got out. Liam watched her approach in silence. The closer Ryan came, the more her son seemed to shine with an ethereal light.

She reached out to hold him, pick him up, take him to safety, and said, "Let's get you home."

Then she woke up. Gasping for breath.

Ryan spent the next day on normal patrol. If anything about this smoky season could be considered normal. The winds remained steady, never forming the redline blow that had worried the fire line. Instead, the breeze kept up a constant sullen rush, carrying an acrid flavor from farther east. The fire station's duty officer called her with regular reports on how the fires had been pushed back from Crescent Valley and one other. Even so, the town did not appear to breathe any easier. All the faces she passed, everyone she spoke with, bore the worry of uncertain days ahead.

She finished early enough to pick her son up from school. A brief word with the principal, an almost friend, who kept a careful eye on Liam; then she drove him home in her police car, even allowed him to play with the light and the siren. Still touched by the tendrils of a dream she did not understand. She seldom remembered

45

anything about her nights. Why this one? And why now? Her son seemed to be doing well, and she had so many other things to worry about.

And number one on that list was why on earth she had invited Ethan Lange to dinner.

She stopped by the market and picked up items for their evening meal, working out her menu as she walked the aisles. Arguing with herself all the while, still uncertain what to do.

As she stood in the checkout line, Ryan finally admitted defeat.

She prided herself on being able to piece together the truth. It was a vital part of her job, being able to assess a situation and determine what was real. And the truth was, Ryan was looking forward to spending time with this man. Something that had not happened in far too long.

And that was what frightened her.

As she stowed her groceries in the trunk and settled in beside her son, she was tempted to call and cancel. Not have to go through the process of introducing another strange man into their home life. It would be so easy to tell Ethan they needed to keep their relationship totally professional.

But the truth was, it felt so good. She liked him. She liked the way others saw him. She liked the flavor of hope. It tasted like a spice from some long-forgotten dream.

Which was when she stopped at a light, looked over at her son, and remembered how it had felt

to come around that dreamtime curve and find Liam standing there in the middle of the road.

"I've invited someone home for dinner."

Liam flashed an instant of fear. There and gone, fast as a single breath.

She went on, "I don't know him very well. We're working together. But he's not really a policeman. Ethan works in a bank."

She started down the central road, taking it slow enough to glance over and see the Christmas lights reflected in Liam's gaze. "Is that all right?"

Liam dropped his gaze back to the sketch pad in his lap. Ryan pulled up to a light and waited. "Liam?"

Finally he nodded. A tiny motion. But clear enough.

"He seems very nice," she said. And waited. But Liam gave no sign he even heard her. Which was typical. She had never met anyone so comfortable with silence as her son.

7

I *have a son."*

The words stayed with Ethan through a long and busy day. Surprisingly so, because the rest of the town seemed trapped in the ash that scattered and flew on another strong desert-dry wind. But Ethan had woken that morning with an idea, one so strong it had brushed aside the creepy fear caused by his final dream's smell and sounds.

"I have a son."

He pushed through the small pile of administrivia and duties that awaited him in the bank, then headed out. He did not talk about his idea, because he wasn't sure if it was even possible. But the sense of having a renewed purpose left him feeling lifted up. He climbed Miramar's central street and enjoyed the sight of Christmas ornaments sparkling in the late-morning sun. He turned off the main road and entered the block containing the city's main offices. Excited. He tried to remember the last time he had felt such a happy anticipation at Christmas. Years. Longer.

Across the street from city hall, the old fire station had become a collection point for donations to the fire victims. Ethan had seen the placards, of course. One was set on the bank's central station, inviting donations to the fund. But he had not seen it in action before now—the cheerful voices, the piles of clothes, the welcoming embraces, the caring faces. It warmed him immensely to see his town come together like this.

Ethan climbed the city hall's front steps and greeted the two elderly gentlemen rocking on the broad front porch. Listened to them talk about yet another unseasonably dry day. Weather warnings of more hard winds from the east. The fire's proximity to Miramar. All the topics dominating this Christmas season.

The younger of the two was Ross Burroughs, former district attorney, former mayor, former mover and shaker in the Middle Kingdom. Now he had a problem with his muscles, or nerves, the doctors couldn't figure out exactly what made walking so difficult. But his mind was as sharp as ever, and the front porch of city hall made an excellent spot for keeping tabs on the world.

Burroughs greeted him by saying, "Heard you've been out on patrol with Officer Eames."

"Once," Ethan replied. "So far."

"How was it?"

"Thrilling and terrifying. In equal measure." He liked Ross, respected the man's intelligence and how he remained determined to stay connected despite a failing body. Ethan leaned against the

49

porch railing and went on, "Everything about it was so intense. It all came rushing back. I was looking at the ruins of a stranger's house and saw my own. When she dropped me off last night, Ryan asked if I wanted to go check out my home with her today. I told her I couldn't. Not yet."

Only then did he notice the woman standing just inside the office's shadows. Adele Shaw's official title was city accountant. Typical of small-town officials who were both trusted and capable, Adele's duties went much further. She was responsible for all the tax rolls, the property valuations, building permits, code inspectors.

Adele asked, "What brings you here today, Ethan?"

Ethan found himself glad to address the two people together. Ross and Adele shared an intensity and a willingness to make Ethan the very center of their hour. He wondered if this had always been their manner and he was only noticing it now. If this change to his perception was the result of losing everything. Being stripped bare. Exposed to the ash and the day.

Ethan swept his arm eastward. "A lot of the homes between us and the fire are owned by outsiders. People who come when they can. Vacation homes. Retreats from the outside world."

"Got to be close to half nowadays," Ross agreed. "They take worn-out farms and the ranches without well water. Turn them into megamansions that stay empty . . ." He noticed the way Adele was frowning at him. "What?"

Adele was small and intense as a whippet, a narrow woman with a voice and spirit strong enough to silence the hardest contractor. "I asked Ethan why he had stopped by. Did I ask you for your opinion? No, I did not."

"I was just agreeing with the man."

"Well, agree with him in silence."

Ross tilted his head. "Was I ever married to you?"

Adele snorted. "I'm happy to report that is one agony I've been spared."

"I was just wondering, since my wife is the only person who's allowed to speak to me that way."

"Consider me her stand-in. And behave, else I'll banish you from the porch." She turned back. "Go on, Ethan."

Ethan described Ryan finding the raw wound in the blackened wall, the missing safe, the furrow dragged through the muck. "Her idea is to get there earlier. Go straight in with the fire crew. Try to beat the robbers, catch them in the act."

"Porter stopped by this morning and mentioned it," Ross said.

"By lunchtime, the whole town will know," Adele agreed. "News about this fire spreads faster than the ash."

"If you manage to arrest those people, it'd be

best to lock them up somewhere else," Ross said. "Texas, maybe. Or Hawaii. Someplace where our folks aren't given a chance to get more riled up than they already are."

Ethan continued. "It seems to me, Ryan's plan might get somebody hurt. Pressing the fire chiefs to let us go in before it's safe. What if we alert the absent homeowners to the threat? Offer them the chance to have us collect their precious articles, store them in the bank?"

Adele and Ross exchanged a look. She asked, "The bank has room?"

"That old structure is built on a pair of over-sized cellars. One serves as our staff room and records storage. We could clear the other one out, fashion some sort of security-lock—"

"What you need," Adele said, "are the county records. Who owns what."

"Man also needs to know where these absentee owners are based when they're not here," Ross said. "Can't do anything without that."

Adele glared at the old man. "You trying to tell me how to do my job?"

"Somebody has to."

"You really are a nasty old coot." She then said to Ethan, "You go on about your day. This could take a while."

8

The evening breeze did not bring any notice-able relief to Miramar. Every time Ryan returned to the kitchen sink, she saw a sky clotted with smoke that threatened to descend and take hold of the town itself. The sunset was a dismal smear of lighter gray. Ryan tried to tell herself she was only doing what most of the town's citizens did with their free minutes, turn eastward and squint and fret. But the gathering dusk seemed especially oppressive. As if the world was determined to smother the season.

Then she spotted Ethan.

Their apartment complex was a series of six two-storey buildings that were constructed in a mock California-country style, with exposed beams and broad balconies shaded by the over-hanging rooflines. They encircled a paved cul-de-sac, with a trio of mini–skateboard ramps and two basketball courts. Ryan had loved the place at first sight.

Ethan carried a bottle of wine in one hand and flowers in the other. The complex's forecourt was almost empty this evening, the kids pushed inside by the smoke. Ryan stood by the window and thought how different this slender man was to her ex.

Ryan had spent her college years loving her former husband's strength and speed, on and off the football field. They were both kids from families who serviced farms and machinery around the nowhere town of Mendota, the nation's cantaloupe capital. Her ex's power and barely controlled fury gave him a full ride to UC Davis. But it was Ryan who studied, while her ex partied and skated through classes as only a winning athlete was allowed. Their junior year, she got pregnant, and he decided he wasn't ready for a kid and a settled life. His child support came directly from the athletic department, which also arranged for her to finish her degree in criminology. Two years later, the child support stopped altogether. His only connection to this incredible son of theirs was the occasional postcard. Even so, Ryan could not bring herself to hate the guy. She was who she was today, mother to a great son, cop in a wonderful town, at least partly because of him.

Strange that she would find herself thinking of the man who had deserted the newly pregnant student. Stranger still how the sight of Ethan standing there in front of her apartment building would make her heart skip a beat. Or bring such a smile to her face.

Then she watched as Ethan dropped to the ground, so fast she worried at first that he had suffered a heart attack. Like most cops, Ryan had witnessed those awful moments after a stroke or sudden illness brought down the formerly strong. She had gazed into the eyes of people who felt the coming change, seen the helpless terror, and done her best to let them know they moved toward the unknown with a friend by their side.

But not today. She felt her breath freeze as the flowers and the wine were released from his grasp. Then she managed, "No!"

Liam called from the other room, "Mom?"

"Stay there!" She raced for the front door, down the central staircase, and out the main exit, flying now, only to be halted by Ethan standing slowly, his hands cupped by his chest, the wine and flowers forgotten.

Then she realized she was still barefoot. And the ash covering her front walk was cold. And it had stained Ethan's trousers from the knees down.

She moved forward and saw what he held. "It's a baby bird."

"No, this is a teenager. See, his mature feathers are coming in."

The thing was impossibly small, a tiny fragile bundle, unmoving. "Is he dead?"

"Not yet. But close. See the movement of his chest?" Ethan started toward the front door. "We have to hurry."

As soon as they entered the apartment, Ethan asked for a medicine dropper and water and unrefined sugar. He greeted Liam by lowering his hands far enough for the child to see what he held. Then he asked Ryan to hurry, it might already be too late.

Liam vanished and swiftly reappeared with a dropper Ryan thought she recognized as coming from her expensive nighttime facial. She started to protest, but then decided otherwise. "Wait, let me rinse that."

"Hurry." Ethan kept one finger on the little bird's chest as he accepted the dropper. "You have his feed ready?"

She passed over the cup. "You didn't say the proportions."

"Doesn't matter if he won't drink."

He filled the dropper, then slipped his forefinger under the bird's head and lifted it a fraction, so as to fit the needle-like beak inside the glass.

The bird gave an electric start and the eyes opened wide.

Ryan saw Ethan breathe through pursed lips. Tense. Worried. She found it incredibly moving, how anxious he was over such a tiny bird. He said, "He's drinking."

The bird spread his wings halfway, flattened his body to the towel, and craned his neck upward. Ryan and her son laughed as the tongue flitted inside the tube. Ethan said, "I've seen this before. I think it might be how the baby bird reacts when he's fed."

Liam's face was inches from the bird. "He's saying thank you."

Ethan nodded. "It does look like that."

Ryan tried to recall the last time Liam had shown such a delighted interest in anything, especially in the company of a stranger, and came up blank.

"Will he live?"

"We'll know soon enough." Ethan glanced at her son. "A bird this young, it's touch and go. You understand?"

Liam nodded, his eyes on the bird.

"Hummingbirds are very vulnerable to smoke. Their hearts beat over a thousand times a minute. Their lungs are tiny and very fragile."

Liam looked at him. Really looked. "You like them a lot."

"I went through a lonely time. They became my friends."

Ryan found herself immensely touched by how the man spoke to the boy. Like they had been friends. For years.

Liam craned even closer to the bird, worried now. "Is he . . ."

"No, he's sleeping." Ethan set down the dropper and continued to run one finger along the bird, from head to tail feathers. "We need to feed him every ten minutes for the first four hours . . ." He looked up. "I left the wine and flowers in the front yard."

"I'll get them," she said.

As she started for the front door, she heard her son ask, "How do you know it's a boy bird?"

"See the gold feathers under his beak? That means he's a guy bird. This is a rufous-crested coquette, one of the most common varieties found in central California."

Ryan hurried downstairs. Smiling at nothing in particular.

After she returned to the kitchen and put the flowers in water, Ryan pulled out a mixing bowl and lined it with her only silk scarf. It was a long-ago Christmas gift from a grandmother who refused to accept that Ryan was the kind of woman who wouldn't be caught dead wearing it.

There was no question of dining at the table, already set with her best china. Instead, she enlisted the two men and together they shifted everything to the counter. They ate by candlelight, pausing every ten minutes to wake the bird and feed it, the duties twice taken over by Liam. They dined on lamb crusted in garlic and thyme, one of her favorite dishes, with roasted potatoes and other root vegetables, which her son positively adored. Their conversation was languid, easy, and surprising. Ethan was apparently very comfortable with Liam's silence. He seemed to respond to her son's unspoken questions, and described waking to the flames and the pounding on his door, the explosion of his workshop's gas canister, the race down the fire-lined road.

When they were finished and the dishes stacked and coffee brewing, Ryan excused herself. As she returned from the bathroom, she heard her son ask, "Are you another deadbeat dad?"

She should have rushed into the kitchen and snapped at him. She should have done a dozen different things. Instead, she froze there in the dining room and listened as Ethan replied, "No. We didn't have kids."

"But you're divorced."

"The week before Christmas." Ethan held to the same easy tone. "Six years ago."

"Didn't you want kids?"

"I did. She . . ."

Something about the way he hesitated caused Ryan's eyes to burn. As if he counted her son's intensely personal and impolite questions as important. It was the most her son had spoken all day. Perhaps all week. She heard Ethan continue, "She said she did. But now I think it was probably a lie."

"She lied a lot?"

"My ex would probably say she was telling me what I wanted to hear. And wishing it was true. For me."

Ryan had no idea whether her son actually understood. But he liked the way Ethan took him and his questions seriously. She was certain of that. She heard Liam say, "My mom used to call my dad a deadbeat. Then she stopped."

"Probably around the time she figured you were both listening and understanding."

"I already did, though. Understand."

"Yes. I imagine you did." Ethan's phone pinged. "Time to feed our hungry beast."

"Can I do it?"

"Of course." There was a pause; then Ethan said, "Your mother tells me you like to draw."

"A lot."

"Will you let me see?"

Another pause, this one long enough for Ryan to assume her son had jerked his head through the rigid headshake that almost always followed her own such requests. And Ethan was searching for another topic. Instead, Liam asked, "Is that enough?"

"Wait until he closes his eyes. Okay. He's full."

The stool scraped, and her son left the kitchen and passed by her and headed down the hall to his room. She was still standing there, wondering what on earth had just happened, when he returned with a sketchbook.

Ryan took that as her cue to enter the kitchen. This, she had to see.

Liam climbed back onto his stool, knelt, and opened the sketch pad on the counter between them. He leafed through the first several pages until Ethan said, "Slow down."

"I want to show you my favorite."

"But I want to look . . ." Ethan went quiet because Liam kept turning. Page after page.

Ryan stepped close enough to watch the images as they came fleetingly into view. The faces, the settings, the battle scenes, the detail penciled in with incredible precision. Ethan appeared to have stopped breathing, which touched her deeply. She liked the intensity he gave her son's work. She liked how he respected Liam. She liked . . .

"Here. This one."

She knew the image only because she had studied it while Liam was at school. He had left the pad open on his desk, which she had taken as silent permission to look. She often begged for a chance to study his work. Do so with him. As much for the bonding moment as to see his work. But Liam rarely allowed himself to be there when she looked. If she tried to tell him how impressed she was, he would lower his head down to where she could not see his expression. Then, soon as he could, he left the room.

Just like now.

"This is incredible," Ethan said. "What is it from, a video game . . ." He stopped because Liam closed the book, slipped down, and left.

When it was just the two of them, Ethan asked, "Did I upset him?"

"I don't know. Sometimes he just . . ."

Ethan nodded. "Drifts away."

She heard a door click shut, knew Liam was gone for the night. "He's talked more with you than he has in, I don't know, months."

Ethan studied the empty space on the counter until his phone pinged, signaling time for the next feeding. Once the bird had dropped back off to sleep, Ethan picked up the bowl and said, "Perhaps I should go."

Ryan did not object. She gathered the sugar solution and dropper in a shopping bag and followed him from the apartment. They descended the internal staircase and exited the building in silence. Ethan stopped on the front portico, studied her a long moment, then said, "This is the nicest evening I've had in a very long while."

"Eating dinner at a kitchen counter, interrupted every ten minutes by a bird."

He started to say something, but remained silent.

"What?"

"If Liam asks, tell him I'll have the bird with me at the bank. He's welcome to stop by after school and help feed him."

Ryan followed him down the front steps and watched him slip away. Walking fast, his footsteps light, a tall man carrying a mixing bowl into the starless night.

9

The star of the morning was, of course, Ethan's bird.

Everyone who entered the bank was brought over and introduced to the tiny beast, who was either feeding or asleep. At least, he remained like that until late morning, when the bird decided he had enough of his silk-lined captivity and went for a little spin. Which, of course, halted all activity through the entire bank. A flash of gold and russet and brown, fast as winged hope; then back he came, landing on the bowl's edge, and looking up at Ethan. Clearly, very pleased with himself.

Ethan offered his finger, and the bird inspected the massive digit, then hopped over. Drawing further *ooohs* from the people now crowding around his desk. If the bird even noticed the throng, he gave no sign. Ethan fed him, settled him back on the scarf, and watched as he fluttered those incredible wings and slept.

"Show's over," he declared.

As the bank's employees and clients reluctantly departed, the bank manager asked, "You stayed up all night for a bird?"

"Nighttime feeds scale back to every ninety minutes. I've helped raise a couple of these little fellows before." Ethan stroked the russet feathers. "I don't mind."

"You sound like a new daddy," Dolores said, and patted his arm. "You are a very sweet man."

The vet's nurse arrived then, bearing a packet of nutrients, a plastic mixing container, and a syringe they used for feeding baby birds. The nurse mixed the supplement in with Ethan's sugar water, then waited around with half-a-dozen other people, who all supposedly had more important things to do. Finally Ethan's phone chimed and he nudged the bird awake. Which was apparently the alert most of the bank's staff had been waiting for. As they gathered once more, Dolores said, "Your little guy needs a name."

"We'll leave that up to Liam," Ethan decided.

"Who?"

"A friend." He nudged the bird with the syringe's tip, but the bird showed no interest in eating. "Something isn't right here. I'm switching back to the dropper."

The bird went from bored to electrified alert. He poked his beak into the dropper and the tiny tongue went to work. Which was when Ethan realized his portion of the room had gone dark. He glanced at the faces now encircling his chair. "Little space here, folks."

By midday, Ethan became aware of a trend.

People arrived worried, harried, their features creased by the same dark smoke that erased

64

Miramar's sky. They walked into the bank, saw the bird, watched it fly, heard the tale of Ethan's rescue . . .

They smiled.

Ethan grew increasingly certain he was missing something. A key element there in these faces, these lighthearted moments, this bird . . .

The day continued.

Lunch was a sandwich eaten downstairs in the bank's ready room, one of the two old cellar vaults that had not seen regular service for decades. Ethan carried the bird down with him. After eating his own meal, the bird went for another mini-flight before conking out. Adele Shaw, the city accountant, arrived in time for that tiny show. Once the bird was asleep, and the offer of coffee refused, Adele asked to speak with Ethan privately.

He led her back to his desk. "It's best to do any private business in the public eye. Otherwise, people will talk." He set down the bowl, seated himself, and gestured at the distant ceiling. "All the hard surfaces in this place, it echoes worse than a cave."

"Works for me." Adele offered him a thumb drive and a slip of paper. "I didn't ask, so I can't say for certain, but I've probably broken a few city codes, putting this list together."

"I won't say where I got it," Ethan promised. "To anyone."

"If it works, you save these folks from losing their treasures, nobody around here is going to mind a bit." She indicated the drive. "Our files are saved according to districts, and the codes won't mean anything to you. Which is why I've given you my phone numbers, office and cell and home."

"Hopefully, I won't have to bother you."

"Honey, we all wish that. Now listen up." She pointed to lines of handwritten numbers and letters. "These are the four outlying districts that contain the Crescent Valley and those to either side. You best start your calls in those areas."

Ethan ushered the diminutive accountant out the front doors, returned to his desk, fed the bird, and resumed work on bank documents. Then a smiling Dolores stepped up and announced, "You have a visitor. He doesn't have an appointment. He says he would have called ahead, but he just got out of school. He's hoping you might make time."

Ethan tracked back to where Liam stood by a grinning bank guard. "Don't just stand there, show the gentleman in."

Dolores held the wooden gate open. Liam walked into Ethan's open-sided domain, seated himself in the chair Adele had vacated, dropped his book bag on the floor, and announced, "I want to borrow a thousand dollars."

10

Ryan was seated in Porter's office, attending the twice-weekly briefing by Maya Ricardo, the deputy fire chief. Maya was a hard-faced woman in her fifties, with a voice roughened by years of smoke and flame. Maps were tacked to Porter's office wall, latest weather reports were lined up to either side, and arrows tracked the fire's next expected assault. That was how it seemed to Ryan. They were not prepping for another patrol. They were readying for battle.

When her phone buzzed, she checked the readout, saw it was Ethan, and excused herself. But once she was in the corridor outside Porter's office, she had trouble understanding exactly what she was hearing.

She finally interrupted him. "Back up there, sport. You're telling me Liam walked into the bank and asked you for a loan?"

"No. Well, yes. But that's not the point."

"What could possibly be more important than Liam asking you for money?"

"The reason why he came in."

"Saving birds."

"I wish you could hear yourself. This is your son we're talking about. The kid who rarely speaks. Only now he's totally caught up in this idea of his."

"You sound, I don't know, excited."

"It's a good idea, Ryan. Really, really good."

"Run that idea thing by me again. I blanked out after you said my son wants a loan."

"We need to lure the hummingbirds out of the valleys under fire threat. We can't go out there and invite them in."

"Obviously." She felt a faint tingle at her heart level. So odd, so totally new, she had no idea what to call it. "I mean, we're talking about birds here."

"Exactly. Hummingbirds can't be shepherded. You know, like they were goats or something. They're very independent. And something else. They are extremely territorial."

There was the background noise of clattering trolleys and people chatting. "Where are you?"

"Safeway. Our third and final stop in this crazy shopping spree. Walking the aisles. Spending money."

"You're loaning my son a thousand dollars?"

"No, Ryan. Of course not. Can I please go on?"

She realized the duty officer was watching. The older woman mouthed the words *Everything okay?* Ryan turned away. The answer was, she had no idea. "Sure thing."

"Okay. Where was I?"

"Territorial."

"Right. So we're going to set up as many

68

hummingbird feeders as we can on that side of town. At least, that's where we're starting. I've spoken with the vet I used for my birds. You know, before. She's putting in an overnight order for another twenty feeders."

"Wait . . . What?"

"We're going to spread out, moving farther and farther into town. Drawing them away from the smoke. At least, that's the plan. Hang on a second." There was the muffled sound of busy shoppers, and then she heard her son say something about nutrients. Her son. Talking with a man who was just one step away from a total stranger. "Okay, I'm back. What time do you want Liam home?"

She tried to work through the swirl of disjointed thoughts and half-formed worries. "Dinner is at six."

"So we'll aim for five-thirty. That okay?"

"Ethan . . ."

"What?" When she didn't speak, he said, "I'm standing at the checkout counter. I need to explain to the lady why we've cleared out all their feeders. And our bird is waiting out in the car, and we're eight minutes past feeding time."

"Okay," she said. Defeated. "Bye."

Hummingbird feeders came in a variety of shapes and sizes. A few generic types could be used in a pinch, but not all. The birds did not perch to eat.

Instead, they hovered, their wings flashing gold and blue and russet even in the dim light, beneath the veiled Miramar sky.

Ethan faced a number of unexpected problems in setting up his first line of feeders, starting with how to mix over a gallon of sugar, water, and nutrients. Then there was the vexation of how to attach the feeders to low-hanging branches. He had twine, but had forgotten to buy a knife. And, of course, there was the problem of how to convince an entire neighborhood to let them decorate their front lawns with plastic feeders.

In the end, however, it proved to be no problem at all.

A trio of interconnected streets, shaped like long crescent moons, framed the town's shopping mall, supermarket, and mini–industrial estate. The houses were mostly old and unassuming. Their yards and old trees and wide front porches were now festooned with Christmas lights. The neighborhood positively glowed.

The district shared an unkempt park, where kids of all ages played a noisy game of soccer. Barking dogs ran interference. Moms sat on benches rimming a sandbox and swing set, watching their toddlers and chatting.

The first two homes Ethan came upon were silent, shuttered, and minus any Christmas ornaments. He pulled up in front of the third home and said, "I need to ask permission. You want to come along?"

Liam spoke for the first time since leaving the Safeway. "I want to hang feeders."

"If we start walking through people's yards without asking permission, we will definitely raise a stink." Ethan opened his door. "Hang tight, I'll handle this."

But in the end, the situation resolved itself. Before Ethan reached the front door, two of the women from the park were hurrying across the street toward them. One of them pushed a stroller, the other held an infant in her arms. The woman carrying the baby asked, "Can I help you?"

As Ethan started explaining what they wanted to do, two things happened, both of which helped. Liam emerged from the car, pulled a box from the rear seat, and drew out a plastic feeder. At that very same moment, the fitful wind pushed a dark skyborne river over Miramar. The two women glanced upward, clearly frightened by how the afternoon suddenly slipped into a gloomy early evening. One of the young mothers broke in, saying, "How can we help?"

"Those poor birds," the other said.

Liam walked over and declared, "He's awake. And he's hungry."

Which meant the mothers watched and cooed over their bird. Apparently, the wide-open spaces held no interest, or perhaps it was the distinct taste of old smoke that lingered in the air. The bird refused to emerge from his scarlet nest. When Liam finished the feeding, the bird gave them a long inspection, then settled and snoozed.

That was all it took.

Mothers were called, and they brought over some of the youngsters. Soon Ethan and Liam had more volunteers than they could use.

He and Liam were relegated to unpacking the feeders, filling them, and pointing to the next house in line. Midway through, they ran out of twine. The last half-dozen feeders were hung using Christmas ribbons.

Ethan and Liam packed the empty containers into three large garbage bags supplied by one mother, while other ladies and kids pestered Ethan, begging him to let them help hang more the next day. The first mother proved to be a born organizer. She took over making a list, arranging details, promising to serve as neighborhood organizer whenever the vet's shipment arrived.

As they drove away, Liam hung out the window, waving a happy farewell. The bird's bowl was strapped in the rear seat, nestled between the last two sacks of nutrients. There was a small rise where the crescent-shaped streets joined with the main road into town. Ethan pulled over to one side and angled the car so they could look out the side windows. Back behind them, the

Christmas lights formed a silent defiance against the gray and the gloom.

"Take a look at that," Ethan said. "Tell me what you see."

He did not expect an answer. And he was not disappointed. Liam stared out his open window, silent. So Ethan said it for him. "Almost two dozen feeders. Hung and filled and waiting to help save the little feathered beasts."

Liam glanced at him. Solemn. Then back to the window.

In the distance, Ethan could just make out feeders reflecting the colored lights. "How did it happen? Because you talked to me. In the bank, of all places. Just walked in and plunked yourself down and told me about a plan you came up with all by yourself."

Ethan settled back behind the wheel and drove away. When the neighborhood vanished into the dusk and gloom, he glanced over, watched Liam play with a blue holiday ribbon that someone had tied around his left wrist. "Why are you so quiet?"

Liam took so long to reply, Ethan suspected the child's silence was the only reply he would receive. Finally he said, "It's safe."

"Safer than what?"

"If I talk, they laugh at me."

"I understand." And he did. "One more question. Don't they laugh anyway?"

The question was clearly unexpected. Liam glanced at him. Shrugged. "I guess."

"See, the thing is, people are worried."

"You mean, adults."

"Right. Your mother is especially concerned. But you know that already, don't you."

"I like the quiet."

"So do I." He gripped the wheel, driving slowly, feeling his way. "I've always preferred silence. A lot of times, words seem like smoke screens to me. Ways people use to hide who they really are."

Liam was watching him now. Which Ethan took as a good sign. He went on, "But sooner or later, you're going to have to learn how to communicate. And do so with ease."

"I can't."

"You can't now. But you can work on it. You need to. It's either that, or you'll find your silence becomes a barrier. It will hold you back. It will keep people out."

"What's the matter with that?"

He saw how Liam's features constricted, and realized the child was struggling not to weep. "Whatever you want to do with your life, how-ever you want to spend your days, it requires being able to talk with people."

Liam used his sleeve and wiped his face. "But you said you like the quiet."

"I do. And when other people start talking a lot,

I usually shut up. But I needed . . ." He took a breath. Remembering a beautiful lady who drew him out. Made him feel like the most special person in the world. And broke his heart in the process. Leaving him so alone, he found comfort in his quiet little birds.

Liam said, "What?"

Ethan had to think hard to remember what he was trying to say. "I needed to learn how to talk when it was important. And it's important you try and talk with your mother. Let her in. She needs that. And so do you." He halted at a stop sign, long enough to see Liam's features had again become a placid mask. "Will you try?"

"Let me see if I've got this straight." Carol Wright worked hard to suppress her laughter. Remain stern and sober. As befitting the chief's wife. "You invite Porter's newest part-time deputy to dinner. Which is a nice move, by the way. Porter thinks the world of him."

"Carol . . ."

"Wait. I'm not done. So Ethan shows up, drops his flowers in the dust, and brings you a baby hummingbird."

"You're forgetting the wine."

"Wine and flowers lying there in your front yard, and he meets your Liam, holding this nearly dead bird. And what happens next, but your son *talks* to the man."

"His exact words were 'Are you another dead-beat dad?' "

"Ryan, I have known Liam since birth. And I can count the number of times he's spoken to me without going beyond the thumbs."

"It gets worse. Liam showed Ethan his drawings."

"Hang on a second. I need to pick my jaw off my chest."

"Tell me." She had the phone on Bluetooth, so she could use both hands to prepare dinner. "Which brings us to today's little astonishment."

"Your son walking into the bank and asking for a thousand-dollar loan."

"So he can buy feeders and try and draw the birds away from the fire."

"I have to tell you, Ryan. The idea has a lot going for it."

"You should have heard the way Ethan described it. He was . . ."

"Tell me!"

"He was happy." She tested the frying pan's temperature by dropping water. When it bounced and spattered, she lay out the tuna steaks to sear. Three of them. "It wasn't like Ethan was doing this to please me. He was happy, Carol. Being with my boy. Making Liam's idea into something real."

She gave that a longish pause. Then, "Where are they now?"

"No idea exactly. Somewhere to the east of town. Hanging hummingbird feeders."

"You know what I'm going to say."

"Don't you dare."

"When I asked about Ethan, Porter said he was a special case. Now I know what he meant." Another pause, then, "The man might be—"

"Stop right there!"

"A keeper. Just saying." Silence. "Well?"

A car she didn't recognize pulled into the apartment building's visitor space. Her son hopped out, reached back, came up with the bowl. Ethan rose from the driver's side, searched the windows, spotted her, grinned, and waved; then he pulled out a pair of hummingbird feeders.

Ryan said, "I have to go. My boys are back an hour early."

11

Ryan did not give Ethan a chance to refuse her invitation to dinner. Instead, she merely informed him he was staying and then ordered the pair to go wash up. Liam emerged dripping water from his face and hands and shirt, as usual. Ethan offered to help, was clearly relieved when she told him to sit down. Not even trusting him to pour the wine. When she set down the plates, he said, "Salad Nicoise? Really?"

She understood his surprise. "My little man will eat almost anything."

"No anchovies," Liam said. "I hate them."

"That makes two of us."

"And Liam's fish has to be cooked all the way through. I hope you like your tuna well done."

"I don't understand sushi," Liam said, and fit a trio of green beans into his mouth.

Ethan smiled across the table, and stayed that way, watching until Liam lifted his gaze and nodded. The boy stopped long enough to return the look. Ethan redirected his smile at her. "Well done is fine."

Ryan asked, "Will somebody tell me what is going on?"

Ethan described their arrival at the park, how

the neighborhood moms and older children had turned their exercise into a mini–mob scene. "We were finished in no time flat." He watched Liam set down his fork and slide off the chair, heading out. "Wait just a second, little friend."

Liam reluctantly halted. Head down. Waiting.

"What did we talk about?" Ethan's voice was very gentle. " 'Dinner was very nice, Mother. May I be excused?' "

Her son repeated the words in a robotic drone. But still. She leaned over, pulled Liam close, hugged him. Hard. Wishing she could do the same to this remarkable man. "Get into your pj's, then come watch TV. No homework tonight."

Ethan knew Ryan intended to ask what was going on, why he had spoken to her son as he did. He also knew there was a very real chance the lady police officer would not like how he had taken upon himself to correct her child. Ethan Lange, stranger, inserting himself where he was not welcome.

Soon as Liam left the room, Ethan said, "I need to ask your help."

"Ethan . . ."

He leaned forward. Pressing against her tide of questions. "This can't wait."

Telling Ryan his plan took no time at all, or so it seemed to Ethan. By the time the table was clean and the meal's remnants stowed, she was with him, already intent on next steps. He disliked watching her slip from motherly hostess to police officer, even though he knew it needed to happen. With the transition, Ryan seemed to become more solid. Stronger. As if the focused intent was so powerful, it included subtle changes to her physical body.

At her direction, Ethan took up station at Ryan's narrow desk by the side window. He inserted Adele's thumb drive into her computer and split the list of houses inside the red-flagged districts. He printed out both sections.

"I'll take all the foreign-owned properties for myself," Ethan said. "I'm hoping the bank will cover the cost of these calls. But they have to be done. Soon as they're taken care of, I'll help you with the others."

Liam was sprawled on the floor to his right. He'd made a nest of sofa cushions, two throw rugs, and a blanket. A CGI-animated film Ethan vaguely recognized played on the television. "*Zootopia*," Ryan said. "I can recite the dialogue line by line."

Ryan worked at the dining table, her chair angled so she could observe both boy and man without moving an inch. She was clearly being shifted to voice mail, and swiftly adopted a quick and efficient patter that Ethan did his best to mimic. Ryan introduced herself as a police officer, then explained she was calling because their home risked being caught in the approaching fire line. She then offered her own and the bank's help in gathering precious items and storing them in a cellar vault set aside for this very purpose. She closed with the station's main number. Over and done in ninety seconds flat.

His own list contained nineteen names and their European addresses. Nine o'clock in the evening, Miramar time, was just approaching daybreak in Europe. All but one of the addresses were for legal offices or trust representatives. The office voice mails repeated their introductions in several languages. Ethan did his best to mimic Ryan's approach, but spoke more slowly. Dictating his message, offering his own number, closing with the same invitation for them to call the Miramar police station for confirmation.

He had just turned to the second of three pages when his phone rang. A heavily accented male voice asked in precise English, "With whom am I speaking, please?"

"My name is Ethan Lange. Senior vice president of Central Coast Savings and Loan."

"A pleasure, Mr. Lange. Bernard Croix here, returning your call from Brussels. I am aware that the hour is late in Miramar. And it is very early here. But the fire will not wait. Correct?"

"Absolutely."

"I thank you for your call. Actually, that does not go far enough. Your message, sir, was a Christmas miracle."

Ethan looked at Ryan and smiled. "Thank you, sir."

Ryan asked, "What is it?"

He covered the mike. "Our first hit."

Croix went on, "I am an advocate and responsible for a number of family trusts. Several of my clients are unwell. These clients, they own seven properties in your region. The sheriff's office does not return my calls. The caretaker has fled."

"How can I help?"

"This caretaker was responsible for all seven homes. I am thinking you should clear the valuables from all those properties. That is, assuming the owners will feel the same sense of urgency as I do."

"That's why I called."

"Can you assure me the valuables will be safe?"

"Our bank is one of the oldest structures in Miramar. There is an underground cellar that will be fitted with a new door. No one except myself or the bank president will enter the chamber. All property will be noted in a special register, and only handed over to a family member or official—"

"Enough. Good sir, you don't know, you cannot imagine, what this call means. I must obtain permission to pass along the gate and alarm codes and numbers to the safes. Excuse me for asking, if the electricity is out, how will you get in?"

"Hang on a second." Ethan lowered the phone.

"I feel like such a dodo. I never thought to ask how we enter the properties when there's no power."

She smiled. "Yes, Ethan. I know how to pick a lock."

Ethan decided her rare smile deserved a longer look. Then, "Sir, that should pose no problem."

"The caretaker had keys, of course. But he has vanished. All seven properties are empty. I will be back to you as soon as possible, good sir. And thank you."

Ryan ran through her list with natural efficiency and finished with him. He sat and watched as she cut off the television and bundled up her son and led him half-asleep to bed. When she returned, the Brussels attorney had still not called back. He rose and said, "Thanks for a great evening."

"Unexpected all around. I still need the long version of your afternoon together . . ." She stopped and frowned at the window. "Oh no."

"What is it?"

"Come see." When he joined her, she pointed to the string of Christmas lights rimming the parking lot. "My early-warning system."

The lights shimmered and danced in the rising wind.

12

Ethan followed Ryan down the main stairs and out the front doors. They stopped there on the portico and stared eastward, into the swirling dark. The wind was a physical force now, and carried the acrid flavor of new flames. Ethan could almost see the valleys under threat, the fragile ridgelines that perched with helpless fear above the rising fury.

A strand of Ryan's hair whipped him in the face. It carried a shocking intimacy, this unexpected touch. Ethan turned from the night and felt her intensity, her power. He was filled with a sudden urge to kiss her. Feel the strength in this incredible woman, claim it for a brief instant. He had not known such a desire in years. It unsettled him, realizing how close he felt to this woman and her son.

Then she broke the spell. "We might as well gear up."

Ethan stepped back. "What about Liam?"

"Amara is a neighbor, and one of my closest friends. She's been my on-call sitter since he was still in diapers."

As if on cue, a hefty woman in her late fifties stepped through the next building's doorway. She called out, "Hakim said he could taste the ashes over his steak."

"Can you come?"

"Be there in ten."

Ethan said, "Ask her if she'd mind feeding the bird. Every hour. Liam will show her what to do."

Amara smiled and nodded in response to Ryan's request and waved them away. "You two go save the world."

Ryan headed up her stairs, pausing only long enough to tell Ethan, "Your place, twenty minutes."

By the time they arrived at the forward station, Ethan's former fatigue was gone. His blood was adrenaline rich now, his thinking as fast as his heart rate. He remained in her vehicle, as she instructed, and watched her stand among a cluster of weary firefighters while the duty chief used both hands to frame the map.

Ryan was both attractive and arresting, especially now with her strength and iron-hard determination on full display. Hers was, Ethan decided, the sort of face that could save a man's life, then discount it as a normal part of her duty.

His attention was drawn away by the chiming of his phone. Ethan wondered how he managed to have a signal until he spotted the portable comms tower rising from an equipment truck. He recognized the number as belonging to Noah Hearst, the Hollywood set designer.

Ethan answered the phone. "I can explain."

"Oh, good. Because for somebody who claimed to be interested in my new project . . ."

"More than that. I'm hooked."

". . . You are one hard man to pin down."

"I've been incredibly busy." Ethan's explanation was cut short by a Klaxon, so loud it might as well have been in the car with him.

Noah demanded, "What was *that?*"

Ethan watched teams clamber into their vehicles and set off. "I'm at the firefighters' base of operations."

"Say that again."

"I've been deputized." Swiftly he summed up what he and Ryan were doing.

Noah responded with a moment's silence, then, "Okay. As far as excuses go, that one's not bad."

"It's also the truth." Ethan saw Ryan turn his way and wave. "I have to go."

"Ethan, wait."

"What?"

"Be careful." Noah's former good humor was gone now. "You're an artist. A good one. Maybe the best. We need you alive and intact."

"I'll call you when I can." As he slipped his phone back in his pocket, the entire forward station became bathed in a brilliant glow, strong enough to halt all movement, all conversation.

A ridge cut from the night sky suddenly erupted. A dark line ran down the hillside, like an invisible ravine. In an instant, the trees to either side of the dark streak caught fire. The great flaming pillars punched the fire straight up, only for the cinders to be curved and twisted by the high wind.

Ethan was drawn from his vehicle by the sight. A faint roar greeted him, a rumbling rush of fury he felt in his chest. The swirling cinders joined over the dark strip, forming a cathedral of flame. Then the tide shifted, pushing the fire into a great river of destruction, carried by the wind.

Ryan walked up, calm as ever. "There goes the fire line."

She drew him over and introduced him to Maya. He watched as the two women and several crew bosses huddled over a series of maps. They discussed the night in terms that sounded like a new language. *Incident management, team admin, type three AHIMT, the alpha side, complex incident* . . . Ethan listened as they broke the fire down into seven sectors: front, rear, both sides, top, bottom, interior. He heard them respond to radio traffic that to his ear sounded like panicked garble. He saw how Ryan was one of them. Calm and resolute. Determined to save all they could.

He had never felt more of an outsider.

It was almost dawn before the firefighters gained a new foothold against the flames. The wind died as the light grew, and weary foot soldiers trucked in for coffee and hasty meals and new orders, and a few for bandages. This time, when Maya directed them back into town, Ryan did not object. The situation was clear on all the faces surrounding them. The fire's status was too uncertain for them to proceed.

As Ryan drove them back toward Miramar, Porter's voice came over the radio, asking for a sitrep. Ryan described the situation in ten seconds. Less. Porter responded, "A house alarm just went off, next valley over. You're closest by five miles. Can't raise the sheriff."

"We'll check it out."

Porter read them the address and signed off. Ryan said, "I should have asked if you minded. But it wouldn't have mattered if you did. It's us or the call goes unanswered."

"That address is on my list."

It took Ryan a moment to realize what he was saying. "You're sure?"

Ethan nodded. "One of seven managed by that Brussels attorney. Who never got back to me."

Dawn had strengthened by the time they started down the road winding along the valley floor. Ryan pulled into the drive to find the electronic gates had been forced open. They were bowed and bent like a broken mouth. Ryan radioed the news, switched on the spotlight attached by her door mirror, and unsnapped her pistol. When they pulled up in front of the house, she said, "Stay here."

The mock ranch house was single-storey and

built of stone and exposed beams, a lovely place despite the shattered front door. Ryan approached carefully, her weapon held down by her right thigh. Ethan found the sight both disturbing and intensely magnetic. Ryan wore her game face, all tight angles and strength, as she pushed the door open and entered. His chest locked as she stepped from view. Ethan remained unable to draw a decent breath until she reappeared and waved him forward.

The house was a miserable wreck. Robbers had taken what they could and left ruin in their wake. Furniture slashed, tables and chairs broken, mirrors and windows shattered, a futile rage that mocked the fires and left Ethan deeply shaken. Just the same, he used his phone to photograph each room from various angles. When Ryan saw what he was doing, she held up her mini-camera and said, "I need to be the one shooting the evidence photos."

"These are for the Brussels attorney," Ethan replied. "Soon as I have a signal, I'm sending them."

"Good idea. If that doesn't light a fire, nothing will." She lowered her camera. "Sorry. Bad pun."

"Terrible."

"You're smiling, though."

Soon as he could, he emerged and stood in the strengthening daylight. Taking great breaths of the smoke-laden air, when . . .

A dog appeared at the home's southeastern corner. It was a breed he did not recognize, a miniature sheepdog whose caramel coat was layered and stained with ash. It danced into view, whimpered, and stood there, shivering and ready to flee.

"Easy, girl. Easy." Ethan lowered himself to where he knelt in the ashes. Extended one hand. He heard footsteps scrape inside the shattered door. "Ryan?"

"Here."

"Grab a bowl and fill it with water."

"On it."

Ethan remained as he was, one hand outstretched, murmuring softly, trying to draw the dog forward. Ryan returned, lowered herself, and set the bowl just beyond Ethan's reach. Frightened as she was, the dog could not resist the need. She slunk forward, panting softly, and began to drink.

Ethan slowly approached, until he was close enough to stroke the dog's shivering flank. He checked the collar tag and said, "Her name is Sable." Then he corrected himself. "Probably pronounced Sablé." He accented the last syllable. "It's what they call butter cookies in Belgium."

Ryan knelt beside him and scratched the dog between her ears. "Okay, I'm impressed."

"My ex was French Canadian."

The dog finished drinking, studied them a moment, then retreated.

"Here, girl. Don't . . ."

Sablé slipped back around the house. Returned. Barked once. Waited.

Ethan rose and followed her.

They rounded the house to discover a stable attached to a small barn, and beyond that a corral fitted with small training jumps. Sablé paced nervously by the stable doors, back and forth, whining softly.

Soon as Ethan pushed open the doors, the dog flitted inside. They entered the shadows, lit up their phones, and scanned the interior. All the stalls appeared to be empty, their gates left ajar.

Ryan said, "Let me go first." She walked slowly down the central passage, back to where the dog stood, panting softly. "Ethan. Come give me a hand."

He walked back to where bales of hay were stacked, and discovered a furry bundle of kittens, so young some of them still did not have their eyes open. Only then did he hear their faint mews.

Ryan handed him her phone, pulled a saddle blanket off the side frame, and squatted in the dust. "Without their mother, I doubt they'll survive."

Ethan spotted a shadowy figure slipping down steps leading to the hayloft. "Here she comes."

The mama cat dropped the mouse she was carrying and hurried over, but made no protest as Ryan bundled up her babies. "Six. Come here, sweetheart, let's get you to safety."

Then the dog barked.

Ethan swiveled his light around and discovered the dog standing by the rearmost stall. He walked back and discovered . . .

The sight was so unexpected, Ethan experienced a moment of electric fear. Like he had come face-to-face with an apparition, one drawn from deepest shadows.

"Ryan."

She stood, her arms filled with a blanket and furry beasts. "What?"

"You've got to see this."

A newborn foal lay in the filthy hay. Its spindly legs were tucked in close to its body. The coat was purest white, an impossible color in this dismal place. The mare stood directly behind her newborn, a beautiful creature of dusky gold, with a mane of gray frosting. She observed Ethan's approach with calm, trusting eyes.

Ryan said softly, "I could shoot that caretaker."

13

The fire chief radioed twice to warn them the wind was picking up and the fire was headed their way. Ryan insisted on staying put until Porter arrived, and Ethan did not object. She phoned her sitter, explained the situation, thanked the woman profusely for getting Liam off to his final day of school before the Christmas break.

Ethan found stashes of dog food in the kitchen pantry, but nothing for the collarless mama cat. Ryan filled the horse trough with fresh oats, while Ethan put out a bowl for the dog, then opened a can of tuna fish and set it on a plate next to the mewling babies.

They located a horse trailer behind the barn and hitched it to Ryan's patrol car. Ethan resurrected a coffeemaker and two intact mugs from the kitchen debris and made a fresh pot. He brought the mugs out to where she sat on a hay bale, feeding the mama cat from her fingers while the kittens nursed. She pointed to where Sablé lay sprawled in the shade. "She went through two bowls of dog food in no time flat."

He handed her a mug. "There's no milk. Sorry."

"Doesn't matter." She took a sip, sighed, sipped again. "You tired?"

He settled down on the cat's other side, began scratching her between her ears. "I'm weary in my bones, but not the least bit sleepy."

"Adrenaline rush will do that to you. It's why so many officers go straight from patrol to the bar. Only way they can sleep is to knock themselves out with a double dose of booze."

"Not you?"

"Once. Yeah. My early days. Now all it takes is a long look at my son. All the knots just ease away."

Ethan rose and walked back to check on the mare and her foal. He returned, settled, and stroked the cat between her ears. Ryan liked that about him, how the man was so comfortable with silence. It was a lesson she had been forced to learn, living with Liam. Nowadays the endless chatter some people used to fill empty spaces left her uncomfortable in her own skin.

The mama cat stopped eating and began licking her babies, long strokes with her tongue, head to tiny tail. Ryan rose and walked to the stable's open doors. In the dim smoke-shrouded dawn, she found herself free to dream. It was something from her younger days, back when her high-school flame was still her champion, the hero of her heart. Back when they shared a passion for running wild. Back when dreaming of happy days to come was just another birthright.

Porter arrived half an hour later, with the sheriff

and the county's lone evidence-gathering team in tow. Together with Ethan, they loaded sacks of feed and the mare and foal in the horse trailer. Sablé followed and settled on a canvas sack of oats. The cat and her babies went on Ryan's rear seat. Porter called his wife, then told them, "Carol's thrilled to bits with the idea of having a new baby horse to raise." Porter stared at the dog panting and watching them. "I guess we can make room for Sable. Doesn't appear she'll give us much choice."

Ethan said, "Actually, the name is pronounced—"

"I heard what you and Ryan called her. But I don't do French, and neither does Carol." He addressed the dog. "You better jump when I bark."

Ryan asked, "What about the cats?"

Ethan said, "I called the vet. She's got a list of people willing to help with animals orphaned by the fire."

They left for town soon after, taking it very slow. Ryan had never pulled a horse trailer before, and worried more than she probably should have at every curve and bump. Ethan called the bank, apologized, said he was taking the day off. When the town-limit sign came into view, Ryan flashed her lights and Ethan waved a vague hello.

They stopped by Porter's home and watched his wife and daughter croon over the foal, welcome the mare, stroke the dog's pelt. Ryan was filled with the tight adrenaline jolts of a long night on duty. Even so, she felt good, and from the smile that never left Ethan's face, so did her ride-along. When she suggested they stop by the diner for a late breakfast after leaving the kittens with the vet, Ethan readily agreed.

The diner's fragrances greeted them, strong as a shout. Ryan was accustomed to the sudden onset of hunger following a hard night. Ethan was caught utterly unaware. She had a quick word with the owner-cook before seating herself. Their order was rushed through: Spanish omelet, grilled tomatoes, home fries, the works. They did not speak a word until both plates were empty. When they were done, and the plates shifted to one side and their mugs refilled, Ethan said, "Cop cars serve as confessionals. That's what you said."

"Sort of, yeah."

"What about diners?"

"Oh, absolutely." She settled back. "Fire away."

"My wife is French Canadian. I mentioned that . . ." He caught her sudden smile. "What?"

"You just said, your *wife*."

He blanched. "Did I really?"

"Not something I'd make up. Believe you me."

He studied his mug. "I must sound so pathetic."

Ryan resisted the sudden urge to reach across, grip his hand, hold it until he was there with her again. "You're coming off a hard night. You get caught up in the moment. Past and present meld

96

together. *Pathetic* isn't the word that comes to mind."

Ethan remained silent and motionless for so long, Ryan suspected that was all he had to say, until, "All the while we were together, I felt as though I lived with two ladies. The woman she was, and the person she tried to be."

"For you."

He nodded. "Aurelie loved me in her own way. Enough to try and make it work. After she left, her friends liked to say how they were relieved it was over, how I should be too."

Ryan did not even try to hide her bitterness. "I've heard a few such snide comments myself. Back in my own awful days."

Ethan continued to address his mug. Nodding slowly. Remembering. "Not to mention their expressions, their eyes, the oh-so-sympathetic smiles. How Aurelie was back where she belonged. And in a way, I knew they were right."

She leaned back. No longer needing the feel of his hand to be connected.

"Our home was Aurelie's one chance at a quiet life. A stable relationship. A husband who didn't play around." He lifted his head, stared at the window. "A kitchen garden. Two parakeets. Little niches carved in the walls to hold the miniature houses I made for her."

Ryan did not realize her throat had closed until she had to force down a swallow.

97

"The other Aurelie . . . She used to say it was because of how she had been raised, a lone child in a home with a revolving door for relationships. But down deep, I think I knew, even then. This was what she wanted for herself as well. This was who she was."

"The woman who couldn't be what she wanted to be. For you." Her voice sounded tight in her own ears. "But that doesn't make a lie of her love." Ryan met his gaze, felt the man's power and sadness both. It gave her the strength to complete the thought, say what had happened to her own former true love. "It broke her heart to take that other course. It twisted her soul. I doubt she will ever recover."

14

Ethan paid for both breakfasts and followed Ryan from the diner. He could see Ryan was concerned for him, he knew he should say something to assure her that he was okay. Which he was. More than that, actually. The caring way she had responded to his breakfast confession left him feeling almost whole.

She stopped on the sidewalk, searched his face, and said, "Maybe I should take tonight's shift on my own."

"Not a chance." Which was when the idea struck. "When does Liam get home from school?"

"Usually between three and three thirty. But today marks the start of school holidays. It could be earlier."

"Tell him I'll pick him up at four." Her response was a fractional jerk away, and instantly he knew he had been wrong to say it as he had. "Ryan, I'm sorry. I'm tired and I didn't think that through. I should be asking your—"

"Liam is very literal. Four means four. Five past means he is disappointed." She gave him a dose of that hard-cop stare. "I try hard not to disappoint my son."

Ethan did not walk from the diner so much as

drift. His thoughts spun in the gray-tinted sky like fireflies. Repeatedly he returned to what Ryan had said, the way she gripped him with her gaze and hand and words. He had never known anyone to speak of Aurelie's departure in that way. Or how their divorce might have impacted her. Certainly not his own mother, who had adored the woman and assumed their breakup was all his doing. The quiet man who could not adjust to the brilliant light that Aurelie had shown her mother-in-law. The perfect wife, the ideal daughter-in-law. His mother still spoke of Aurelie's absence with genuine sorrow.

Miramar's old town opened on his left, with the restored neighborhoods of early homes and the stately city structures. He took the right-hand turn into the section thrown up almost a century later, when Miramar's sons returned from the Second War. He passed two other houses needing a rebuild, properties he had watched with a restorer's patience, waiting for the chance to bid. Ethan stumbled on the uneven pavement, his energy flagging to the point where lifting his feet higher proved difficult. He pushed himself up the front steps, stripped as he walked back to the bathroom, and stood in the shower until the hot water ran out.

But when he lay down, as he sighed his way out of the weary hours, a recollection jolted him back to full wakefulness.

• • •

The last time he had seen Aurelie had been there. In the diner. He stared wide-eyed at the bedroom ceiling and tried to recall if it had actually been in the same booth as the one shared with Ryan.

Three years back, the week before Christmas, Aurelie had phoned him out of the blue. Middle of the week, working at his desk; a call transferred back. The day suddenly transformed by a blur of conflicting emotions. She was in town, had driven down on a whim. Could she buy him lunch?

Sitting across from her, listening to the sparkling conversation that had framed their happiest hours together, the air had tasted like champagne.

Her words had washed over him with the memories and the yearnings, an orchestral melody of her own making. His heart had flashed with the old desires that he had assumed were lost and gone forever. Until that very hour.

Ethan let her order for them both, as often happened whenever he was enveloped by her magic. When the waitress departed, she reached for his hand, and she looked at him. It became just another wondrous hour, spiced with a hope he knew was a lie, even when his heart beat its untimely race, and his loins burned with the passion of earlier hours. Her magic was that strong.

Then her phone pinged.

Aurelie had always kept it nearby. She was an ER nurse, the profession she was born for. But even in the heady days when he remained willfully and stubbornly blind, he knew the hospital was not the reason she was so swift to turn the phone over and read the incoming text. Just like now.

Her face changed to one of elfin delight, a timeless jolt of pleasure and abandon, the emotions too strong for her to hide. And there in her features, that other person was abruptly revealed. The life where he was not welcome, and would never belong.

He knew it so well.

All the heartbreak he had known surged back into being. All the reasons he had finally walked away from the only woman he had ever loved.

Ethan rose and stood there beside the booth, imprinting her image into his heart and mind. Then he said, "I can never see you again."

He had left the diner without a backward glance. And all the way home, the sparkling Christmas decorations and drifting holiday music had mocked his broken state.

15

At first glance, the afternoon merely limped forward. The alarm woke Ethan at half past two. He rose feeling as weary as he had when lying down. He made coffee, dressed, ate a meal he scarcely tasted. His body still ached from the long night, his thoughts were foggy, his heart sore from the diner and the memories that followed.

And yet . . .

The sense of floating stayed with him. Ethan pulled into the circular lane fronting Ryan's home to find Liam sitting on the building's front steps. He cradled a mixing bowl and was surrounded by a bevy of curious kids. They reluctantly made way when Liam stood and started for the car. Liam settled the bowl in his lap, clipped his seat belt, and waited. Like they had been doing things together for years.

Ethan asked, "How's our patient?"

"He doesn't always sleep after he eats."

"That's a good sign. It means his strength is returning." Ethan glanced at the upstairs windows. "Where's your mom?"

"Still asleep."

"If anyone in Miramar deserves a day off, it's her." He texted Ryan that he'd picked up Liam, then said, "First coffee. Then the vet. Then we go have a treat. How does that sound?"

Tired as he was, Ethan could not help but notice the coffee shop's charged atmosphere. Several people he did not recognize smiled at his entry. Everyone seemed to watch as he responded to the server's cheery greeting and ordered a coffee. Curious.

Ethan drove east from the town's center, past the commercial center. On the town's outskirts, he turned into the first line of buildings behind the mall. One of these, a sixties-era house, which had been built cheaply in the first place, had been redesigned as the vet's office. It was an almost-perfect location, with ample parking and a wide lot that now held a large air-conditioned unit for her patients. To the vet's right was the town's new feed-and-tackle store. To its left was the vet's home, another nearly derelict residence she and her partner had bought for almost nothing and turned into something almost stylish. Beyond that stretched three wooded acres with a rotting FOR SALE BY OWNER SIGN nearly covered by vines and fungus.

The vet was a compact woman named Piper Vinson, a no-nonsense lady in her early forties. She was universally adored by her patients, and she loved them in return. The same could not be said about their owners. Animals in pain or severe distress were welcome 24/7. But woe be it to any owner who interrupted Piper's off-duty hours with anything that she deemed not an emergency. When angry, Piper could blister paint at twenty paces.

Piper's front yard was sheltered by tall California Coulter pines. As they rose from the car, a gentle wind hummed a melody that Ethan loved. It was a big reason why he had lived in one of Miramar's eastern valleys, so the whispering eucalyptus and pines could greet him on so many dawns, and share with him the close of days. Only now . . .

He lifted his face to the afternoon sun. Not believing his senses.

"I taste salt."

Then he heard someone call from the vet's front porch, "The wind has shifted!"

The words were enough to bring Piper bouncing out the front door, followed by several owners and their charges. She took the same pose as everyone else, nose pointed to the sky, searching.

Then she spotted Ethan. She pointed in their direction and shouted, "Ladies and gents, the rock stars have arrived!"

Piper came bounding over. "You must be Liam." The vet jerked her chin at Ethan. "This old guy you're spending time with, he's weird, but I'm pretty sure he's harmless."

"Excuse me. *Old?*"

"Borderline ancient. Right, Liam?" She poked Ethan in the ribs. "I definitely heard a squeak there. Didn't you, young man?"

"Nope."

She poked Ethan again. "Definitely."

"Ow."

"I'll give you 'ow.'" To Liam. "I've got a large-bore needle in there, long as your forearm. It's supposed to be for cows and horses, but it might perk up Mister Ancient here."

"No needles. Large bore or otherwise."

"Then you better behave. Right, Liam?" She pointed at the house. "The kitties and their mom all appear in tip-top shape, but they've been through a lot, so I'm keeping them close. I've had a dozen or so little girls and their mothers telling me they want a baby kitty for Christmas."

Liam added, "Mom says I can't keep one."

"Well, seeing as how your mom is a cop, I guess we better do what she says. Where's your little feathered beastie?"

"She means the bird," Ethan said.

"Quiet, you. Liam and I are having a conversation here." Piper tracked the boy over to the car, followed by what appeared to be her entire clientele.

Liam pulled out the bowl; Piper leaned over to inspect, then snapped, "Give the doctor and patient room to breathe, why don't you." But the crowd only shifted back a smidgen. "Definitely male, looks like you're doing a good job here. What's his name?"

"I like . . . Trevor."

"Trevor's good." She stroked the bird from beak to tail. "Always loved these little creatures. They're so full of life it gives me the shivers."

Ethan only gave the exchange a small part of his attention. Mostly, he kept testing the air, checking how the nearest branches began leaning in tandem, as if every tree within sight shared his giddy disbelief.

Piper glanced over and smiled. "Grand, isn't it."

"Is that . . ."

"Rain. Smells like it to me."

One of the men offered, "Weather report claims it's not lasting beyond this afternoon. Tonight it goes back east and blows—"

"Shush, you." Piper kept stroking the little bird and told Liam, "We'll take any shred of good news on offer. Won't we, Mister Hero."

"Why do you keep calling me that?"

Piper straightened. "Because that's what you are. Ask anyone."

Ethan decided it was time to say, "We've come for more feeders."

"Hey, I'd like to help and all, but we're fresh out."

Her smile was disconcerting. "You didn't get the shipment?"

"Oh, absolutely we did."

"I don't understand."

"Clearly."

Ethan realized her grin was now shared with everyone within hearing. "Piper—"

"I told you, I'm having a conversation with our young hero. So stop interrupting." She squatted down, placing herself at Liam's eye level. "Young man, the whole town is talking about you two. How you came up with the idea to save my absolute favorite birds in the whole universe. And how this creaky old guy has been out saving kittens and a beautiful dog named after my favorite cookie and a baby horse and her mother. Which has absolutely made my day, I don't mind telling you."

When Liam seemed incapable of responding, Ethan asked, "So the feeders . . ."

"We've had a train of people coming through here. Taken all I had, and ordering about a hundred more. Not to mention stripping my little shop bare of nutrients. All these people you see here, they're wanting to help." She rose to full stubby height, but kept her attention on Liam. "Take in other rescued animals. Dogs, cats, horses, whatever. Including any unicorns or forest fairies this old guy and your mom happen to find."

Liam looked at Ethan, the question mark clear in his gaze. Ethan replied, "She's kidding about the unicorns."

"Only the tiniest bit, little man. And only

because you two have given us all a reason to smile." She touched Ethan on the arm. "Walk with me."

She waited until they rounded the building to say, "If the wind holds to this direction, maybe we won't have to stay up nights worrying about all the orphaned beasties. But whatever happens, you and the boy have given all the animal lovers around here a new reason to hope."

Ethan had no idea how to respond.

She clearly liked his silence. "The first time you came by here, that was what, five Christmases ago?"

"This makes six." Then he recalled, "It was another baby hummingbird."

"When you walked in, dragging your sorry behind, wearing that just-shoot-me expression, I wasn't sure you'd ever climb out of that grave you were digging." She patted his arm. "Glad to know my patient is doing so well."

16

Ryan woke at half past four, and for a long moment, she could not understand where she was. The apartment was silent, still. At some point, she must have woken up and cut off her phone's alarm, which had been set for one. In time to be up and mobile when Liam returned from his final day of school. Instead, she padded through the apartment, calling his name, wondering how she could be such a terrible mom.

Then she thought to check her phone, and found three messages from Ethan. They were simple things, just a few words laying out the afternoon's progress. The first was, he had picked up Liam at ten minutes to four, and they were headed to the vet's. The second reported on how all the feeders had been taken by others, and Piper had called her son a hero. The third had arrived ten minutes earlier, and said they had decided to celebrate with ice cream at the Sundae Shoppe, and she should come join them.

She made coffee and drank it, standing in the kitchen, re-reading the texts. Ignoring the seven from the station and one from the chief himself. Captivated by how wonderful it felt, how absolutely magnificent, to have a good man care for her son. Recognize the qualities that made Liam so special, but remained hidden beneath his quiet manner. This was not simply a man seeking to get on her good side. Ryan was as certain of this as anything in this weird and smoky season. Ethan cared for her son. And she . . .

The hand holding her mug began shaking, the tremors growing to where she needed to set it down. Try and gather herself. Because the truth was there in the gray misty light beyond her window.

She was falling for Ethan Lange.

The afternoon held a wintry chill when she left the apartment. Her car was beaded with moisture, something that happened almost daily in a normal December. Today, however, it was a treasure.

The air was thick and the light shrouded. The wind was backing now, gradually turning to the east, and lingering smoke added an oily taste. Even so, she felt the first faint hope that the worst might be behind them. If only the wind did not rise again from the east. If only the fires were brought under control before more homes and valleys lost.

Ryan drove slowly through town, catching glimpses of upturned faces, clutches of people turned toward the unseen Pacific. Hoping the winter storms were on their way. Despite the weather reports, despite the warnings of more unseasonable desert winds, despite everything.

She passed the ice-cream shop and spotted Ethan with her son in the window table. Ethan was talking, while Liam spooned some chocolate glop and watched him. She liked everything about the scene. Ethan was not forcing himself to make conversation. He was enjoying Liam's company. And Liam was responding in his own quiet way, intent and happy. She was sure of it. She drove on, her joy feeling like a welcome lance probing her heart. Willing her to waken from the emotional slumber of years.

The police station was what Porter called Christmas quiet, when all the normal troubles and crimes took a seasonal break. Or so they liked to pretend. Knowing it wasn't really so, but loving the way it sounded. Maud, the front-office duty sergeant, was the only person in the building. She greeted Ryan. "Porter's been looking for you."

"I slept in."

"No reason not to." She went back to typing. Maud was a wonder when it came to office paperwork. She had spent eighteen years on regular patrol, then switched to the office when her joints started acting up. Now she served as office manager, typed most of Porter's reports, handled all state and federal forms, and maintained an almost-military order to their station. Ryan shared Porter's dread of the day the lady might decide to retire. She went on, "Apparently, all the bad guys decided to take the day off."

Ryan's desk was by the southern window, one of four behind the waist-high barrier that framed the main workstation. Unlike the other active-duty officers, Ryan shared Maud's fanatical desire for orderliness. She liked starting every new day with an utterly clean desktop. The bare surface helped her focus upon whatever case required her attention.

Only today there were two stacks of torn pages, scrawled notes, yellow slips, printed emails. "What's all this?"

Maud did not bother to glance over. "You've had a few people wanting to chat."

"A few?" She rifled through the largest pile, did not recognize any of the names. Below most of the numbers, Maud had scrawled the words, *yada yada yada.* Nothing else.

"Maud."

The older deputy continued typing. "Yes, dear."

"Will you please tell me what's going on?"

Maud sighed and rose and sighed again. Like crossing the office was another pain added to her busy day. "These are your calls from last night and this morning. I don't know how I can make it any clearer." Maud planted a finger on the central pile. "These idiots mostly wanted to ask questions for which nobody on God's smoky earth has answers. As in, are we certain their home might burn up, how much will the bank charge them, does it cost something to have their

113

precious belongings picked up, on and on. You wouldn't believe the utter stupidity on display."

Ryan struggled not to laugh. "I'm sure you were your usual comforting self. Offering Christmas cheer to one and all."

Maud snorted. "It's a good thing they haven't invented a Taser I can use over the phone."

"Any of them actually want us to go by their places?"

"Not that they actually came out and said. More like, 'We'll need to give this more thought,' 'Please, can you send a written estimate?' 'What direction is the fire headed?' like that."

"I'm glad I wasn't here."

"Tell me." She thumped the second smaller pile. "These were the calls from overseas. Same dithering, only with accents."

"Anything from a lawyer in Brussels? Croix is his name."

"Yeah, he's in there somewhere. Tried to call Ethan, got voice mail. His clients are not certain what they want to do."

Ryan said, "We shot pictures of the break-in. Ethan sent them to the Brussels lawyer. I'll send them to you, share them with anyone who wants to waste more of your time."

"That should shift a few of those engines out of idle." She pointed to the lone handwritten note, closest to Ryan's phone. "That's the only call you need to respond to, far as I'm concerned."

Ryan read the name on the slip. "Why does Berto Acosta want to speak with me?"

Maud started back toward her desk. "Sounded to me like he wanted to get in on the dance."

The builder greeted Ryan by saying, "From what I hear, you and Ethan are hitting it off."

"Not trying to change the subject or anything," Ryan replied, "but is there an actual purpose behind this conversation?"

Berto's laugh rang over the phone. "How many homes want to store their treasures in Ethan's place?"

"All we've gotten so far is a lot of dithering." She described the break-in, the photos, her plan to send them out. "But that is probably about to change."

"If that happens, I'm thinking you'll wind up with more stuff than you can handle with your cop car."

"What are you saying?"

"I've had a word with Porter. I'm giving you my two best haulers. These are fellows I'd trust with my life. Porter says it's up to you. If you agree, he wants you to deputize them."

"To do what exactly?"

"Bring their valuables to the bank, what do you think?"

She glanced up and realized Maud was smiling at her. The expression was surprisingly gentle for

115

a woman with her years on the beat. "Berto, it's very nice. You do realize our budget wouldn't allow us to pay you."

"Yeah, Porter's already sung me that tune. Call it a Christmas present to the town." Berto was clearly enjoying himself. "So, do we have a deal?"

She made tentative arrangements, thanked the builder profusely, hung up the phone, and said to Maud, "You knew this was happening."

"Whatever are you going on about?" She tried to hide her grin and failed. "You know I tell you everything."

"Liar." Suddenly she wanted nothing more than to go join the boys. Taste some of her son's ice-cream glop. Share their smiles.

Be with Ethan.

As if she could read Ryan's thoughts, Maud offered, "The fire chief spoke with Porter about half an hour ago. Things are looking better. No significant signs of further spreading. And the sheriff's office is taking over this evening's valley patrols."

She gathered up her purse, started to grab the messages, then asked, "You really don't mind sending out the photos?"

"Do I look all that busy to you?"

"Okay, great. If anybody actually gives you the green light, give me a shout."

"Will do." Maud turned back to her computer.

"You be sure and tell our handsome new deputy I said hello."

"I'm sorry, who are we talking about here?"

Maud kept typing. And smiling. "Liar."

When she entered the ice-cream parlor, Ethan was at the counter paying and her son was making a feeble attempt at cleaning the mess off his face. She stood by their table, planted her fists on her hips, and pretended at anger. "I should be out handling all sorts of urgent police business. But here I am, watching my two men ruin their appetites for dinner."

Liam said, "I had chocolate."

"I see that." She took a clean napkin, dipped it in Ethan's water, and began cleaning off the mess. "How did you get ice cream on your shoes?"

"It was fun."

She cleared away the worst of it, then straightened to find Ethan standing there, smiling at her. "You want your face cleaned too?"

"You just called me one of your men."

She started to take it back, but then decided there was no need. Or it was too late. Or something. Instead, she asked, "Do you feel like working?"

"Do I have to?"

"Not tonight. Apparently, the fire is taking a break."

"Then absolutely not."

"Is it too early for you to call Brussels?"

"Ryan, it's the middle of the night over there."

"Good." She looked at Liam. "What should I do with my two men who are not the least bit interested in food or doing anything productive?"

Liam said, "Beach walk."

"Why am I not surprised." Ryan clapped her hands, then shooed them toward the exit. "Beach walk it is."

They took the patrol car, which meant Ryan could slip past all the vehicles circling and searching for a space and park in the EMER-GENCY VEHICLE slot. Exploring the sea walk with Liam was one of his absolute favorite pastimes. Ryan did it as often as her schedule allowed, or rather, she had before the fire. As they started toward the mist-clad waters, she tried to remember the last time they had been down here. But everything that came before the fire felt like years ago. Decades.

Liam skipped ahead, a delicate shadow carved from the pewter mist. The sunset was lost somewhere out there, beyond the unseen ocean. The air was cold and salty-spiced, as only a Pacific mist could make it. People appeared and greeted them softly and vanished again, incomplete figures that slipped in and out of view. Ryan felt every breath carried a special elixir, one she had almost forgotten was hers to claim.

Interspersed along the three-mile promenade were suspension footbridges, with rope handles and strings of fairy lights offering feeble illumination. As their footsteps thudded softly across the first, Ethan slipped his hand into hers.

It wasn't his touch that caused her alarms to go off. Not really. It was how she felt. Easy and comfortable and, well, defenseless. She wanted to relax into the moment, give herself totally to these alien sensations. So much. All the while, her mind was filled with all the old warnings: Never to let herself go again. Never risk shattering the life she had made for herself and her son. Never ruin the peace she had made with her solitary existence. Never again.

And yet . . .

Which was the moment Liam stopped by the bridge's far end, waited for them to catch up, and asked, "Where is Ethan going to have Christmas?"

Ryan heard herself reply, "With us. If he wants."

And Ethan said, "Liam, go on ahead, please. I need to speak with your mother."

She nodded and watched her son become just another shadow drawn in the drifting mist. There was no reason for her heart to suddenly thump in such a disjointed manner. None at all.

Ethan said softly, "The vet called Liam a hero today."

"You said that." She heard a faint tremor in her voice. Which was absurd. "In your text."

"I wish you could have been there. Seen her make a fuss over your son."

"Ethan . . ."

"What?"

"Nothing. It's just . . . nothing."

"I have an idea. Something I'd like to share with Liam. But only if you agree."

She watched him take a hard breath. "What?"

"I think maybe, just maybe, his art could become a way for him to connect with the world, instead of using it as a barrier and holding everything at arm's length."

She needed to hear every word. Take it in deep and think it over carefully. And maybe she had. At some level, below the momentary confusion, perhaps it had fallen into her and would wait for a quiet moment, when she was lying in her empty bed, staring into the darkness. Maybe then it would all come out and she would be able to think clearly. Just then, though, all she could hear, the only thing that registered, was how Ethan was so deeply involved in her son. How much he cared . . .

She felt a current, strong as lightning, course from his hand, streak through her entire being, illuminate the moment with a clarity so piercing, it defied the Pacific gloom. She savored his strong grip, the calloused hand. A builder's hand.

Or an artist who worked with wood, creating a dream come true for a dying child. Or speak with such affection about her near-silent boy.

He asked, "Is that all right with you?"

She needed to say something. Ask him to repeat everything, or tell him to wait until she could think more clearly. But just then, the only thing that seemed remotely right, was to reach up with her free hand, pull him close, and kiss him.

17

Ethan invited them back to his temporary home. In doing so, he took a serious risk, several of them, in fact. Ethan did not cook. Even oatmeal was a vague achievement, because he often forgot he had something on the stove. He trusted his microwave and coffeemaker because he treated them like he did his woodworking machines. They behaved properly, so long as he was careful. But Ryan seemed happy with his offer of a salad. They stopped by the ice cream shop for his car, and off they went.

There was a curious feeling as he opened his front door and ushered them into his miniature haven. He had explained this was meant to be a rental, and was furnished in a very temporary fashion. Just the same, he was offering Ryan a glimpse into his private world. The first time this had happened, with anyone, in years.

Ryan took in the wooden crates holding his clean clothes. The trio of stools flanking the kitchen counter. The empty walls. He waited for her to come back with some comment over how no one should live this way, even for a few weeks, much less for a season. Instead, she said brightly, "Why don't I take over?"

"Be my guest."

So he set the counter with plates for three, fed the bird, then beckoned Liam to join him. This was something he wanted to do with the child's mother in close approach.

He took the next stool and asked, "Have you ever heard of the Elven Child?" When the lad shook his head, Ethan answered, "No reason why you should, they've been out of print for ages. They were seven stories in all, written about ninety years ago. When I was your age, I read the books until they fell apart. I wanted to be that kid." He stopped, struck by a sudden lancing pain.

They were both watching him now. Ryan said, "What is it?"

He shrugged. "I collected first editions of all seven books. Took years."

She set down her knife. "You lost them in the fire."

He nodded. "It hits me like this, every now and then. All the stuff I've lost."

She reached for his hand. Held it a long moment. "Okay?"

"Yes," he said. And it was.

He would remember that meal for as long as he lived.

The three of them sitting there together, perched on stools, with Liam's chin almost resting on the counter. Sharing his childhood passion. The feeling among the three of them so intense the stories came to life for him again.

For Ethan, the telling became a return to earlier times. Hard times, with unhappy parents who seemed only able to communicate with each other through yelling and anger and bitter feuding. Ethan's name became just another weapon they threw at one another. When their hotly disputed divorce began, Ethan went to live with his mother's parents. Looking back was something he rarely did, because there was so little he wanted to relive. Yet now, as he described how the first story began, he remembered a few shreds of the good moments. When his grandfather introduced him to this world inside a tree. When he discovered a realm so enticing Ethan could ignore the shattering of his family.

The first novel, *The Crystal Pipe*, began when a soon-to-be grandmother threatened to cut off her only son from his inheritance unless they name their first child Avariel. Both father and mother had despised the name and all the secrets it carried, so they had always called him Gary.

They raised Avariel in some town north of LA proper, in an apartment, in a tower, deep in the heart of asphalt and crowds. Even so, the young child had loved parks, where songbirds would come and perch on him, long before he could even speak in words. And the parents had observed, and worried.

Their worries grew stronger still when Gary

began running away. Lost for hours, sometimes overnight, drawn away from the city by the song of forests. The parents punished him; they grounded him and threatened him with all sorts of dire actions. Gary tried to explain how the green world called to him. How he loved the quiet and the fragrances and the animals. How he felt at home there. But the more he spoke, the angrier they became.

Then, the winter Gary turned eleven, his grandmother died.

The family estate was a rambling mansion set in many forested acres, and surrounded by a tall stone fence. The grandmother's will left it to her son and heir, but only if he agreed to live there. This was something Gary's father had sworn he would never do. But Gary's father was nothing if not shrewd. He had long suspected his mother had been planning such an absurdity.

Long before the old woman's death, he had put his strategy in motion. The city was booming and spreading and desperate for more space and homes and factories. With the help of hungry builders and their army of lawyers, Gary's father set out constructing a new future.

Yes, they would move to the estate. But on the father's terms. Not the old woman's. The manor would be torn down, the land stripped of forest, and a cluster of big executive houses would be erected inside the ancient walls. An exclusive enclave for the rich and privileged. Part of the city, but safe from its dangers. Perfect.

To Gary, the old woman left a box.

It was very old, the strange carvings almost indistinct, the wood petrified. And inside was a crystal pipe, no longer than his finger, almost like a glass whistle for a dog. Nothing else. No note, no explanation, nothing.

It was at this point that Ryan softly announced, "Liam has fallen asleep."

Ethan half carried, half guided, Liam out to Ryan's car. He settled the boy into the backseat, softly closed the door, then straightened to find Ryan standing. Waiting for her chance to hold him.

Strong arms enveloped him, the woman's breath warm on his face, her lips on his. They shared a timeless farewell. He shut her door, waved at her departure, and stood there watching as she drove away.

18

E than woke soon after sunrise. The fact that his body could have used another couple of hours changed nothing. The dream had come again, just a faint whisper this time. Wings that sounded close enough to brush his face, a tiny hint of smoke in the air, and he opened his eyes.

Mist clung stubbornly to the town, blanketing Miramar with drifting patterns of gray and gold. Ethan walked along a street he could scarcely see. He stopped for coffee, feeling as if he drifted with the fog, barely connected to the earth or the strengthening day. He sat by the café's front window and caught himself smiling in his reflection.

He entered the bank, greeted his fellow employees, sat behind his desk, and began sorting through the previous day's notes and phone messages. Then Dolores walked over and planted herself by the little gate.

"What on earth are you doing here?"

He watched Carl's approach. The bank manager stopped by his head teller as Ethan replied, "Last time I checked, I still worked here."

"That's not what I mean and you know it."

"Actually, I don't."

Carl asked, "When do you go out on patrol?"

"Depends on the wind and if people come back saying they want us to store their valuables." He looked from one to the other. "What is going on here?"

"You don't think the bank can survive the week before Christmas without you?" Dolores seemed genuinely affronted. "Suddenly you're Mister Indefensible?"

"Indispensable," Carl corrected.

"Whatever."

Carl told him, "You are now officially on paid leave."

"What leave?" Dolores said. "He's working the fire line, he's saving people. That's no leave I've ever heard of before."

"The only people I've saved so far walk on four legs," Ethan pointed out.

"We've heard all about that too." Dolores pointed to the front door. "Go rest up for whenever. The bank will be here when this is over."

Carl asked the teller, "Don't you think we should tell him about the party?"

"Not if Mister Incapable here thinks he can use it as an excuse to stick around a second longer."

"I think he's gotten that message," Carl replied. He told Ethan, "We've been talking to the local business owners."

"We, as in everybody here, and more besides," Dolores said. "Because of you."

Carl said, "The town is hosting a pre-Christmas party for the firefighters tomorrow night."

"They've taken over the guesthouse on Ocean Avenue as their rest-station," Dolores added.

"We're setting up in the parking lot," Carl said. "Turkey, trimmings, pumpkin pie, party hats, the works."

"We'll feed everybody in stages," Dolores said. "All the crews get their turns."

"I want to help," Ethan said.

"You *are* helping," Dolores said. She opened the little gate. "Now you just come with me."

Downstairs he found Dolores's husband, a carpenter who handled the most difficult assignments for Berto Acosta, working alongside three younger assistants. They paused long enough to greet Ethan, then went back to fitting out the largest of the cellars. Solid shelves anchored to three walls, better lighting, cleaned air ducts, and a stout oak door with double locks. Carl showed him the podium now planted in the concrete antechamber and explained how only Ethan and Carl and Dolores were permitted entry, how they had to sign in all consignments, how they already had four calls that morning from families near the fire line, how the bank might need to bring the crew back to outfit the second cellar. Ethan was still taking it all in, seeing his basic concept come to such vivid life, when he found himself shooed back up the stairs, down the central aisle, and out the bank's front doors. Dolores saw him off, saying, "You know the word *enjoy*, yes? So go and do."

Carl grinned, said, "You heard the lady." And shut the door behind him.

Ethan had no idea what to do with his free hours. Since long before the fire, he had existed by filling every minute with work of one kind or another. Life had been defined by keeping busy. As if he accomplished a minor victory just in making use of his time.

Now, however, he drifted.

He did not call Ryan, for fear of waking her up. He passed the diner, nixing the idea of another meal. He started toward his house, but at the juncture turned left rather than right and walked into Old Town. When he reached the municipal buildings, he stopped. Now that he was here, he felt as though this had been his destination all along. Even without him knowing.

The old fire station was a hive of activity. One pickup full of donations was being unloaded, while another was being filled with gift-wrapped packages and sacks of clothes and groceries. A half-dozen volunteers in red Christmas hats were busy sorting and folding and preparing goods for distribution. The station's concrete walls were crammed with piles of clothing, food, six-packs of water, diapers, toys. Long trestle tables flanked both sides. Along the back wall, another group in Santa hats gift-wrapped toys and candy and new clothes.

The sense of drifting continued, only now it granted Ethan a distance even from himself. He felt as though his life had contained two different identities. Two lives.

Ethan found it oddly fitting, to be confronting this here. Watching his fellow townspeople do what they could to help the fire afflicted. But it took him a long moment to understand why.

He had lived such an insular life. Particularly around Christmas. Seeing his world in terms of loving a woman who was incapable of loving him back. And then the arid afterlife of recovery.

Six years.

To say it was his fault was worse than useless. He had done his best at the time, or at least thought so.

Two lives.

The *before* was over. This much he knew was true.

Which left him facing a new and unexpected challenge. What was to come now?

To that, he had no answer.

As he started away, Ethan realized what he was seeing.

Four hummingbird feeders dangled from the building's corners. Others adorned the town hall's front porch. Another trio hung from branches of neighboring fruit trees. All of them festooned with Christmas ribbons.

Birds flitted in and out of view, tiny bolts of color and speed, hovering by the feeding tubes, drinking, flashing away.

The sight took his breath away.

19

Ryan called a half hour after he got home. Ethan was at his counter, making a first attempt at sketching the elven village. His drawing abilities were rudimentary, more of an architect's design than anything artistic. But Ethan suspected that was all the initial phase required. He would submit a few concepts, then Harvey Chambers would probably require everything to be redrawn. Someone this captivated by the old tales would have his own set of mental images, carried with him since childhood, potent enough to force his executives to go along with his plan. Invest the network's cash, sell the concept to advertisers, book a place in the network's hottest season. All for a story that had been out of print for longer than Ethan had been alive.

Ryan's first words were, "I should have been up hours ago."

"I'll write you a note."

"Will you? How nice. How are you, Ethan?"

"Fine. Making some initial sketches. What is Liam up to?"

"Amara's pretending to watch a cartoon movie with him. *Beyond the Hedge.* For maybe the twentieth time. That woman's patience is unbelievable." She paused for a sip. Sighed. "You met her. My regular sitter. Liam thinks Amara is great. She has two children, one works in New York and the other in Mexico City. She misses her grandchildren something awful. She and her husband claim Liam is the reason for their happiest hours." Another sip, then, "I try not to be jealous of all the days Amara gets to spend with Liam."

"Is Amara taking Liam all day?"

"Ethan, I just crawled out of bed. My brain is moving at turtle speed. I need one of Piper's horse needles to inject this coffee straight into my veins."

"Why don't I come pick him up."

A silence, then, "Ethan . . ."

"What?"

"Wait, let me ask him." She set down the phone, called, murmured. When she came back on the line, she sounded much more awake. "Liam says yes."

"Great." He grinned at the blank kitchen wall. Ridiculously pleased. "That's great."

"Ethan . . ."

"What?" Another silence. "Ryan, take a breath and shape the words. Please."

"The fire is partially under control. There were two messages on my phone when I woke up. Sheriff's department is super stretched.

They ask if we'll do a drive-by of houses in the surrounding three valleys. Just making sure there haven't been any further break-ins."

"Count me in. But does that leave me time to be with Liam?" When she did not respond, he gently pressed, "You need to tell me what you're thinking. Otherwise, I have no idea what's right in your book."

"We can't leave on patrol until I'm done with a meeting at the station."

"Which means what time, more or less."

"I should be finished before six."

"I'll be ready."

"Ethan . . ."

"Yes?"

"Nothing. It's just . . . Thank you."

"For what?"

She breathed into the receiver. Again. Then cut the connection.

When Ethan pulled up in front of Ryan's place, Liam was again seated on the front steps with a backpack slung over his shoulders and the bird's bowl on his knees. But the hummingbird wasn't in its resting place. Trevor was perched on the boy's shoulder, from where he gave Ethan's approach a bright-eyed inspection.

"Ready to go?"

In reply, Liam offered the bird a finger. Trevor hopped on board, allowed Liam to deposit him back in the bowl. Sat there on his silken nest, watching the world as they walked back to the car.

Ethan started the car and said, "I thought we'd stop for a bite, then go by the vet's and check on the kittens. Then head over to Porter and Carol's place so you can meet the foal. How does that sound?"

"Great."

"Excellent." He started to put the car into gear, then stopped. "I'm doing some preliminary designs for a new project."

"The elven village. For the TV show."

Ethan nodded. "How would you like to do some sketching this afternoon?"

"With you?"

"Right. At my place."

"I don't have my pad."

"I've got a couple of extra sketchbooks."

"And pencils?"

"Many as you need. All colors."

Liam gave him a solemn look. "I'd like that more than anything."

Ryan sat at the head of Porter's conference table. Her boss had the day off, so she led their regular meeting with the deputy fire chief. The walls were covered with survey maps and lists of people and equipment and twice-daily weather and regional law enforcement updates. Exhausted as she was,

Maya did a fairly good job of injecting a bit of hope into her talk. As a result, the table was ringed by rare smiles. There was a new tune being inserted into their weary days. For everyone but Ryan.

The sheriff's report was less positive. Two other houses near the fire's perimeter had been broken into. Ryan was fairly certain one was on Ethan's list. She was tempted to phone him, offer this grim update. But somehow she just couldn't bring herself to insert this news into his and Liam's afternoon.

She rubbed the place over her aching, frightened heart. And wished she could just run away.

Listening to Ethan that morning, feeling the comfortable closeness, drawn in by the smooth quiet manner of this fine man, her terrors had woken up.

There was no way she could deny the truth. She was, after all, a cop. A good one. And one of the crucial traits of being good at her job was that she sought the truth.

Even when it hurt.

Even when it threatened to tear her world apart.

Because that was what was going to happen. When Ethan left.

It was just what men did. Her father, turning to the arms of a woman only four years older than his daughter. Her ex, loving the wild nights of running more than he would ever love his wife

137

and newborn son. She had vowed never to endure another broken heart. Yet now she had broken her oath.

Her mind shrilled a resigned fear. She had left it too late. She should have ended things long before now. Back when she could have walked away and remained intact. Back before her quietly beautiful son had become so bonded to this man.

The assistant fire chief must have noticed her struggle to maintain control, because Maya broke off her summary and asked, "Everything all right, Ryan?"

She wiped her eyes. Nodded. Clenched her entire body down tight. The truth was that hard to bear.

She loved him. Ethan Lange. And it was too late for her to do anything about it.

20

Ethan stopped for take-out burgers at the diner. They ate sitting in the car, the windows down, watching the holiday shoppers stroll past. Daylight came and went, scattering brilliant lances through the drifting mist. When they were done, Ethan drove slowly along the town's main thoroughfare. He felt as if he had never really noticed Christmas lights before. The air still tasted of old smoke, but for once he did not mind.

Hummingbird feeders were strung on lampposts, doorframes, shop signs; slender tubes dangling from ribbons that sparkled as they spun. Little flashes of life, scarcely larger than ornaments on a Christmas tree, darted in and away. Their feathered dance slowed both pedestrians and vehicles. Ethan watched a pair of young girls dance in place and shriek with joy as a hummingbird spun just overhead. He saw smiles everywhere.

He started to tell Liam, when the boy spoke for the first time since they had left the apartment complex. "Will you stay?"

It felt as though Ethan's car slipped into the parking space of its own volition. He cut the motor, listened to it tick, rolled down the windows a trifle more, and sat there. Giving the lad's words the space they deserved.

He did not pretend at not understanding. Nor did he want to deflect. It had surely cost Liam to ask. Ethan knew whatever he said risked disappointing the child. Which he wanted to avoid more than anything.

It seemed as though his silence was the right reaction, for Liam turned from his inspection out the side window. And sat there, so solemn he seemed to shrink down, becoming even smaller than he already was.

Ethan said, "It's too early to tell whether this is real. No, that's not the right . . . I know it's real. But I can't say whether it will last. And neither can your mother."

Liam appeared capable of holding his breath forever, he was so still.

Ethan went on, "I know that's what you want. And it means more than I will ever be able to say. Because I think you are one of the most special young men I have ever met."

Liam used the palms of his hands to dig into his face. Squeezing his eyes, compressing the emotions back inside. Pushing and pushing.

Ethan did not speak until Liam was watching him again. "I can tell you this. Whatever happens between your mother and me, I want to stay your friend."

This time, Liam let the tear streak a tragic line down one cheek. "Promise?"

"This is as real as it gets," Ethan said. "I promise."

He could not say whether he reached first, or if the boy moved. Only that Ethan was the one to take Trevor's bowl and set it on the backseat. Because holding Liam became the reason why he had arms.

They sat like that for the longest time, comforted by each other's closeness. Ethan watched the passers-by and wondered at the mystery of being so incredibly happy and so intensely sad, all in this one mist-clad moment.

Finally it was time to restart their day. Liam released him and settled back, Ethan passed him the bowl, started to turn the key, and . . .

He realized where he had stopped.

"Will you be okay here by yourself, just for a moment?" Soon as Liam nodded, Ethan rose from the car.

Castaways was pretty much the same as he remembered. He had once been a regular, since his ex had loved dressing up and going anywhere fancy, and he had loved the food. And the music, though he had only managed to hear the owner's husband, Connor Larkin, play twice in all the times they had been here. But all that was in the past, and Ethan had not returned in over six years.

The young man behind the hostess station showed no recognition. Or welcome. "Sorry, sir. We're fully booked through the holidays."

Ethan assumed that was why they had positioned this unfriendly guy up front. To turn away people. The restaurant's head waitress was a beautiful and flirtatious lady who loved nothing more than making people happy.

"If it makes any difference, I used to come here a lot."

"Sure, you look familiar." He showed all the interest of a showroom mannequin. "Just the same, we—"

"Aren't you the hummingbird guy?" The head waitress stepped over, hands full of stemware. "Sure. You're him. Where's your sidekick?"

"In the car." Ethan had always had a knack for remembering names. Never had it been more helpful than now. "You're Marcela, right?"

"None other." She turned to the guy on door duty. "This is him. The guy who's out saving birds from the fire. And homes. You and the cop lady."

"Ryan."

"Sure." Marcela glanced out the front door. "That's her kid?"

"Yes. His name's Liam."

"The hummingbird hero. That's what people are calling him, right?"

"You know about that?"

She pointed to the young man frowning behind

142

the hostess station. "Even Carlos the Moaner knows about you. Everybody's talking about you three."

Carlos protested, "Marcela, don't even think—"

"Did I ask you to fuss at me? No, I did not." To Ethan, "You want to bring the lady here for dinner?"

"And Liam."

"Of course and Liam. What would dinner be without the hero?" Marcela bent over the reservations book. Turned the page. "Connor is playing Christmas Eve."

Ethan did not actually speak. More like, he breathed the word *Please.*

Carlos moaned, "Marcela, no, wait, you know what Sylvie—"

"She's not here. And if Sylvie was, she'd say absolutely yes." Marcela kept searching.

The young man planted his elbows on the podium and placed his head in his hands. And moaned.

"Okay, Carlos. Here." She stabbed the book with her forefinger. "Give them table six."

"Marcela . . ."

"Table six, write it in." She beamed at Ethan. "Seven o'clock, one seating, and don't you dare tell a soul I did this."

"I owe you big-time. Both of you."

"That's what we like to hear." She patted Carlos on the shoulder. "See how easy that was."

Carlos moaned again.

• • •

As they pulled into the vet's parking area, Piper bounded from her clinic and started over. She planted fists on her hips and glared at Liam. "See all the trouble you've started?"

Liam stared at the feeders now adorning every tree in Piper's front yard. "They're everywhere."

"Well, of course I had to get in on the act. What choice did I have after your idea took hold?" She smiled. "A lot of people have wanted to do something. But they're 'fraidy cats, like me. Too scared to spend time in the badlands like your pal here."

"And my mom."

"She's a champion in my book. No question." Piper pointed toward the clinic. "Go ask the nurse to show you the kittens. Have her give you one of my Swiss chocolates. No, leave the bird here. What's his name again?"

"Trevor. He doesn't ever go far from his bowl."

"Trevor has survived a very hard time. He feels safe with you. Give the little fellow a chance to get his strength back." She set the bowl on Liam's seat, stroked the bird, then straightened and said to Ethan, "Come with me."

She led him around back, where a concrete-lined depression was designed as an outdoor cleaning and grooming area. "Here, take this."

"This" was a white plastic box, about two feet square, with a hose and a pump sprouting from its top. The contents sloshed as she passed it over. "What is it?"

"What does it look like?"

"I don't . . . A portable shower?"

"See, I knew you weren't as dumb as they say."

Ethan watched her open a large outdoor pantry and rummage around. "Who is 'they'?"

"I forget. Doesn't matter." She emerged holding plastic animal-carrier cages, several leashes, water bowl, and a pair of black insulated gloves. "Grab a sack of that feed."

The bag of dog food weighed twenty pounds, perhaps more. "Piper, what's going on?"

She had already started back toward his car. "That feed works fine for cats as well. If an animal approaches you, it's probably because they're hurt or hungry or both. And filthy. Crouch down at their level, offer them water, then a handful of feed. Let them take the first steps. Don't start toward them unless you're sure they won't bolt. Once they've eaten, clean them off a bit."

He popped the trunk, watched her settle the gear inside. "What do I do with them afterward?"

"Bring them here, what did you think?"

"Piper . . . I have no idea."

"Well, maybe they were right about you after all." She slammed the trunk. "Happy hunting."

Carol Wright took a calm pride in showing them her new arrivals. The vet had stopped by earlier

145

and pronounced both mother and foal to be in excellent shape, especially considering what they had been through. Yes, and the dog, of course. Sable appeared when Carol whistled, along with the family's two Malinois. The dog looked freshly scrubbed and calmly happy, like she had been part of this family for years.

When Porter walked around the corner of the house, he greeted Ethan and Liam with, "How are you two getting on?"

"Good." Ethan watched Carol take hold of Liam's hand and draw him closer to the mare. "Ryan's working."

"Oh, I know all about that. She's handling the day's conferences. I owe her big-time."

"My man doesn't like all the administrivia that comes with his job," Carol agreed. To Liam, "Stroke her up here, between her eyes. She likes that." She reached into her pocket, drew out a pocketknife, took an apple from a bucket hanging from a nail, and cut slices. She handed them to Liam. "Open your hand wide, that's it. Let her feed. Good. Now you can stroke her baby. It's okay, go ahead."

Porter told Ethan, "I try to tell Carol this is a temporary arrangement. I'm not sure she's hearing me."

"They're happy here," Carol declared. She was a handsome woman in her late forties, with a streak of solid iron for a spine. The voice might stay calm, but Ethan suspected it was all for the horse's sake. "They're mine. I'm not giving them up without a fight."

"There's the small matter of legal ownership."

"Possession is nine-tenths of the law," she replied, almost singing the words as she stroked the mare's nose. "I remember a certain police officer telling me that once."

Porter rolled his eyes at Ethan. "That's what they say, sure enough."

"Plus I'm heavily armed. And I know how to shoot."

"I didn't hear that because you didn't say it."

"They come near my baby and her mama, I'll do more than talk."

"Carol."

"I'm laying down the law, Porter. Carol Wright's law."

He started to argue, then thought better of it. He said to Ethan, "You find any more orphan horses, take them someplace else."

Liam settled his cheek on the foal's neck. Stroking the little head. Abruptly the mare fluttered deep in her chest. Liam jumped back, frightened.

"Don't worry, honey. That's a sound mama horses make when they're happy." She shot her husband a look. "Or when they agree with what I'm saying."

On the ride back into town, Ethan raised the subject he had first discussed with Ryan. "How would you feel about drawing something for me?"

Liam tapped the window each time they passed another hummingbird feeder dangling along the street. Ethan assumed he was counting. Now the boy swung around and said, "I thought that was what we were going to do."

"I don't mean, you and I draw together. I mean, you help me with my project."

"The Elven Child. For television."

"Right. Do you remember what I told you about the story?"

"I remember every word."

"How would you like to sketch an idea for the elven king's palace?"

Liam watched him.

"I have to warn you. There's very little chance they will use what you come up with. These people can be very tough about concepts. You design something. I design another. Noah, that's the set designer, he'll probably make some sketches of his own. The executives will probably assign a couple of in-house artists. That's people who work full-time for the studio. They'll do more." Ethan glanced over, trying to get a read on what the boy thought of all this. "But I'll pay you. I spoke with your mom and she says it's okay. I'll give you fifty dollars for whatever you come up with."

Liam watched him awhile, then turned back to the window. Cradling the bowl. The bird resting on his wrist.

"Liam?"

He spoke slowly, as if measuring each word. "I like that more than almost anything."

And that was the last word Liam spoke.

When they arrived back at Ethan's home, they set Trevor's bowl on the kitchen counter and Liam fed the bird. Then Ethan set out two pads and a double handful of colored pencils and felt-tip pens. Liam opened his pad, stared at the blank page for a time, then slipped off his stool.

Ethan asked, "Everything okay?"

In response, Liam carried his pad and a half-dozen pens and pencils across the main room. He deposited them on the floor, as far as he could get from Ethan. He started to kneel, then looked over. Stood and shifted his position so Ethan's view was blocked by his easy chair. As the boy settled on the floor, Trevor popped out of his bowl, inspected the situation, then flew across the room and disappeared behind the chair. When his phone chimed and Liam did not rise, Ethan took over feeding. Every time he walked over for the bird, however, Liam closed the pad's cover and would not meet Ethan's eye.

Two hours later, Ethan said it was time for them to be getting back. Liam shut his pad, gathered up the pens, and set them on the counter. Ethan carried the bowl out to the car. Liam did not offer to show Ethan his work, and Ethan decided not to ask.

Ryan had the apartment's door opened when

they climbed the central stairs. "Did my boys have a good day?"

Liam nodded, endured his mother's kiss, and disappeared inside. Ethan asked, "Does your other boy get a kiss too?"

She smiled, sort of, and pecked him on the cheek. The quiet mystery still visible in her dark eyes. "How was he?"

"Liam was great."

"Really?"

"Yes, Ryan. We've had a wonderful day."

As she ushered him inside, Ethan had the impression that his reply had somehow saddened her. Before he could ask what was the matter, Ryan turned brisk, ordered him to set the table, and disappeared inside the kitchen.

They dined on cold roast beef, potato salad, and wilted spinach. Liam worked his way through everything in his normal silent state. Ryan spoke briefly about her meetings, the slow progress being made in halting the fire's spread, the next day's weather prediction. She mentioned the two new break-ins, and Ethan confirmed one of them was on the Belgian attorney's list. He started to ask for more details, but something in her gaze, a resigned distance, kept him silent.

Mostly, Ryan seemed to be watching them. Studying Ethan and Liam with a sad and intense gaze. Her gaze remained weighted by concerns that she did not share.

Ethan decided not to press. If anyone deserved to carry secret weights, it was a cop and single mom with an untamed fire threatening her town.

When Liam was done eating, he lined up his utensils like little soldiers, and said, "So. The elf king's palace."

"Yes?"

"It's part of the tree?"

Ethan nodded. Remembering. "It's of the tree and separate. That is how the author described the village and the palace both. A freestanding palace, but bound to the tree, like the tree is bound to the earth. And the light and the air and the wind."

"I like that."

"So do I." Ethan smiled at the astonished expression Ryan showed them both. "The impossible made real, that's how the book describes the elven village. Just like the season of Christmas—when all things beautiful on this earth have the potential to come to life. If only we work hard enough. If only we try."

Liam picked up his fork, began drawing on the tabletop. Then, "The elves just live inside the trunk?"

"The book doesn't say exactly. I always thought they're everywhere. Trunk, branches, roots, leaves. But that's just me."

"Leaves fall in winter."

Ethan shook his head. "Remember, the story takes place here."

"Here, Miramar?"

"Farther south. I grew up thinking it was Ojai or Long Beach or somewhere in between. Later in the series, I think it was book five, the tree is named as a Japanese broadleaf oak. I looked it up. It's very rare, but it's real. An evergreen belonging to the genus Quercus. They stay green all year."

Liam drew a moment longer, then, "I don't like the child's name, Gary."

"It's a name for the city, sure enough."

"But his real name . . ."

"Avariel." Ethan could see where this was going. "Once he learns how to play the crystal pipe, he discovers that his grandmother's grandmother was an elf, who fell in love with a human. And ever since, any child who could make the pipe sing was welcome inside the elven world."

Liam gave that a moment. "Avariel sounds like a song."

"That is actually the name of book four, *The Song of Avariel.*"

And just like that, the child was done. Liam set down his fork, slipped from the chair, and started away. Then he turned back and asked, "Dinner was very good. May I be excused?"

Ryan nodded, watched him disappear down the hallway, then asked, "Who is that child, and what have you done with my son?"

21

Ryan put on another pot of coffee and set out two thermoses for the night run. When she started cleaning up, she refused to let Ethan help. So he shifted over to the kitchen counter and watched her move. Quiet, swift, efficient. Lovely to observe.

"Liam was very quiet as an infant. He whimpered, but if he cried, there was always a reason." She washed dishes and set them in the drying rack. "Even when I couldn't make things better, a toothache or a fever, whatever, he stopped crying when I tried to explain. He watched me, just like he does now. Solemn. Aware. Like he already understood. I know that sounds crazy."

"No, it doesn't," Ethan replied. "He understood enough."

"Then he got older, and he still didn't talk. After his third birthday, the doctors started mentioning the most horrible things. Smith-Magenis syndrome, apraxia, environmental deprivation, autism, Einstein syndrome. It scared me to death. Middle of the night, I'm laying there all alone, filled with the worst kind of dread, helpless."

Ethan rose, walked over, and took her in his

arms. She felt rigid, an iron-hard woman who had spent years holding firmly to control.

Slowly, gradually, she relaxed. Flowed into him. Held him tight as breath. Then softly pushed him away. Wiping her eyes. The moment of allowing herself to be fully exposed and needy gone now. Ethan resumed his seat. Glad he had been there to catch her.

"When we were together, just the two of us, all the doctors' warnings and worries, they didn't seem real. Like they were talking about other children they had to deal with. Attaching labels that really didn't apply to my son. Not seeing Liam at all. Just trying to fit him into their graphs and questionnaires, because it kept them from needing to confess they had no idea what was going on."

She started wiping down the already-spotless cabinets. "By that point, I had been reading to Liam for years. Whenever I did, Liam became so intent, so focused. I knew it was more than just the sound of my voice."

"He heard you," Ethan said. "And he remembered."

"All the junk I fed that child. Sports pages, women's magazines, romance novels. I was never much of a student."

"You did fine."

"I even read him . . ." She glanced over, her gaze luminescent, almost smiling.

"What? Tell me."

"Crime scene reports. Texts on pathology and criminal law I was studying for my detective exam. You name it." She leaned against the counter, crossed her arms, smiled at the past. "Soon as I picked something up, didn't matter what it was. He'd take aim. When he was about two, I got him this little rocker, painted the most horrible banana yellow. I cut up an old quilt for padding. He'd snuggle in there and just watch. For hours."

"And listen."

"The feeling to those moments was so beautiful, so intense." She shook her head. "Sometimes I'd keep reading until my voice was nothing more than a smoky rasp. One of those nights, I realized the doctors were wrong. I didn't have any evidence except what was right there in front of me. But I was certain my beautiful little child would start talking when he was good and ready."

"And he did."

She nodded slowly. Kept nodding. "The week after he turned four, he asked me to read from the C. S. Lewis fantasy."

"*The Lion, the Witch and the Wardrobe.* I loved the Chronicles of Narnia series."

"I still have those books. I'll never give them up." She went quiet, then said, "He's never talked with anything approaching ease."

"There's nothing wrong with preferring silence, Ryan."

"A lot of his teachers and fellow students disagree."

"Well, they're wrong."

Ryan glanced at the wall clock. "I want to settle Liam for the night before we go. You're okay here?"

"Ryan, of course."

As she walked around the counter, she slowed, halted. Lifted one hand and placed it on his shoulder. She did not speak. Nor did she need to. Ethan met her shimmering gaze. He felt it in his bones long after she disappeared down the hall.

Three minutes later, she was back. "You need to see this."

He rose and followed her down the corridor. Ryan pushed open a door and beckoned him forward.

When Ethan's eyes adjusted to the gloom, he saw a young boy in Star Wars pj's. Liam had wrestled all his covers up into a tight bundle under his chin. One hand was extended out, like he was reaching toward the two of them, the fingers open and slightly cupped. There on the tip of his middle finger sat Trevor. The bird had his head tucked down, a feathered parody of the boy's position. Asleep.

Ryan slipped her arm around his waist and rested her head on his chest. As if she knew Ethan needed this human anchor to keep him connected to earth. As if she wanted to keep his heart from expanding out so large, it might defeat his ability to keep it all together.

22

Ethan left the house an hour later, as close to whole as he had been in a very long time.

It lasted until he was midway to the car.

During the hours they had been indoors enjoying a meal and a shared affection for a young boy coming into his own, the mist had vanished. A fitful breeze now blew from the east. The distant horizon was aglow. The air carried a heavy burden of smoke.

He started the car, rolled down the windows, and watched the babysitter cross the forecourt and enter Ryan's building. The car's heater could have erased the chill and most of the odor. But the bitter flavor helped him think.

Which was why, when Ryan slipped into the car, he was ready. Almost.

Ryan said, "And here I thought it was the night for dreams coming true."

He gave that a beat, then said, "I've had this faint whisper of an idea. More like a question. What if?"

When she realized that was all he was giving, Ryan smiled. "Not a lot to go on. So let's hear what you've got."

Telling her the tight snippets of an unfinished

idea took two minutes. Less. When he was done, she tapped her hand on the car's roof. Once. Twice. Then, "Make the call."

Nine forty-five on a central coast evening was a quarter to seven the next morning in Brussels. But the attorney had given Ethan his cell, and urged Ethan to phone. Besides which, Ethan suspected the lawyer might be more open to these half-formed questions outside his office.

"Mr. Croix, good morning, it's Ethan Lange. I apologize for calling so early."

"Think nothing of it. I'm already well into my day. What can I do for you, Deputy?"

"What can you tell me about the caretaker?"

"Have you located him?"

"No, sir. To be frank, we've been too busy to look."

The attorney's sigh came at them from all the car's speakers. "Well, to answer your question, I do not know enough, in my opinion."

"Excuse me?"

"Ben Wattell was the live-in caretaker when one of my clients purchased their Miramar home. They decided to keep him on. A year later, the caretaker for three of the other properties retired, and Wattell agreed to handle them as well. Over the years, he gradually took on all seven properties owned by my clients." Bernard's speech slowed. "We talk. Occasionally. Not often."

Ethan caught a new reserve to the attorney's voice. He glanced at Ryan. She continued to frown at him. Intent. Ethan said, "Surely, there must have been any number of reasons to contact the man overseeing properties for a number of your clients."

"One would think so. Yes."

"Sorry, I don't—"

"We communicated. But speaking with this man was . . ."

Ethan waited him out. Watching Ryan. She had the same dark-gray gaze as her son. Big eyes, not quite round. Ethan found himself wondering about all those eyes had seen.

Finally the attorney said, "Frankly, sir, I did not like the man. And the feeling was mutual."

Ryan pulled the notebook and pen from her shirt pocket and scribbled. She showed him the page, and Ethan read aloud, " 'What can you tell me about the original family Wattell worked for?' "

"Nothing at all."

"Because . . ."

"I am expressly instructed to say nothing what-soever. The new owners forbid it."

"The *new* . . ."

"Monsieur Dubois was partner in a textile firm and one of my closest friends. He and his partner, Monsieur Lambert, both decided to purchase their Miramar homes after vacationing there. Two years later, they lost their wives within weeks of each other. More recently these gentlemen also passed away. Heart attacks, both of them. Tragic."

"So these homes . . ."

"Now belong to their respective children."

"Could you—"

"No, Deputy. I could not. I am specifically instructed to say nothing about them. I'm sorry."

Ethan kept his gaze locked on Ryan. The Belgian attorney did not sound the least bit put out by his questions. "I apologize if I've overstepped legal boundaries."

"How else can you determine where the boundaries lie, except by asking?"

Ryan turned to a fresh page, scribbled the word *Cheerful?*

Ethan nodded. "Can I ask something else?"

"Most certainly, you can ask. Whether I am able to answer . . ."

"The residence where we had the break-in."

"Madame Kassel. Yes. Fine woman. Unfortunately, she is now suffering from dementia. Her daughter is now responsible for her estate. As a result, I have recently been placed under the same edict."

Ethan asked, "You can't talk about her either?"

"Correct."

When the attorney stopped there, Ryan began nodding. As if she was urging him forward. Ethan asked, "The instructions not to speak about the daughter, did they come from the same source as those for the other two families?"

"Sir, you have a habit of posing very interesting questions."

"So . . . you can't answer."

"I thought I just did."

"Back to the caretaker. Do you have a current address?"

"Not exactly. Ben Wattell emailed me yesterday, as it happened. He apologized for being out of touch. He has driven to Nova Scotia. The trip required over a week. He has started a new job. He formally resigned."

"And before?"

"Ah. Yes. Mr. Wattell resided in a cottage on the Dubois estate."

"One of the estates that refused our offer of assistance. Now controlled by the next generation."

"Correct."

"So being granted permission to enter the estate . . ."

"Out of the question."

Ryan swept a hand across her throat. Ethan said, "Sir, Bernard, I have taken far too much of your time."

"I'm sorry I could not be more helpful. Might I ask, what is the fire's status?"

"We're about to go find out." Ethan cut the

connection and watched as Ryan drew out her phone and started dialing. "Who are you calling?"

"Porter. He's an early-to-bed kind of chief." She pointed to the road ahead. "He needs to hear this in person."

Porter's response was definite. "There is no way I'm taking this to Judge Mendez."

Ryan did not exactly plead. But she came close. "Chief, come on, this has probable cause written all over it."

"Oh, really. Then obviously I've missed something vital. Because what you've told me doesn't make it halfway there." They were seated at his kitchen table, sharing a pot of fresh-brewed coffee. Porter was dressed in shorts, a vintage Deadhead T-shirt, and fuzzy bedroom slippers. "In total, you've spent less than half an hour on the phone with a lawyer who's legally bound not to tell you a thing. Which means you can't use what he's said in a court of law. Even if he'd given you something solid. Which he didn't."

"He told us a lot."

"He *implied.*" Porter sipped from his mug. "There's nothing here I can take to the judge. Not a single whiff of evidence that would convince her to grant us a warrant."

"Ben Wattell is responsible for two burgled properties beyond the fire line," Ryan said. "He resides on another property—"

"He *did* reside. You have nothing to suggest the caretaker is still there."

"Which is why we need the warrant. To go in and investigate."

"You want to search a home that has forbidden you entry. As is their legal right."

Ethan pointed out, "These burgled properties are both located along the valley where the fire chiefs were certain would be struck next. But the weather reports were wrong, and the wind never picked up."

"Okay, that's a good point. But it's circumstantial. If you had something definite, we could use the weather and locations as extra ammunition. Now, though, it still leaves you searching for a valid connection between the caretaker and the thefts." When they didn't respond, Porter asked, "How did you come up with this in the first place?"

Ryan replied, "It was Ethan's idea."

"Nothing hard and fast, like you said," Ethan said. "But the first time I spoke to Bernard Croix, I had the impression he wanted to say more than he did about the caretaker."

"More than he was legally allowed," Porter said, nodding.

"At the time, I assumed it was because Wattell had vanished when the fires started closing in."

"Even though the estate holding his home is still well removed from the fire," Ryan added.

"Again, circumstantial," Porter replied. "Wattell could have seen the places under his care were threatened, and simply chosen that moment to bolt."

"Come on, Porter," Ryan said. "And then suddenly two of those other estates are robbed just as the fires close in? Really?"

"I'm not saying I disagree with you. But my answer is the same. I need more to get us the warrant." Porter rose to his feet and used his mug to gesture at the door. "Now go out there and bring me something we can use."

23

Berto was good as his word. The two men and their truck waited at the police station for Ryan and Ethan's arrival. Three absentee owners had requested their help removing their valuables and storing them in the bank's cellar. Three from the thirty-one homes on their list, all in the region rimming the present fire line. Ethan was frustrated by their lack of progress and all the unanswered questions surrounding the break-ins. He suspected Ryan felt the same. He could see her frown in every passing headlight. But there was nothing to be gained by discussing it further.

As they entered the first house, Ryan was phoned by the duty officer. She stepped outside, leaving Ethan to shift the contents with Berto's team. As they loaded the truck, Ryan cut the connection and walked over. Her demeanor had shifted to a new level. Tight, almost angry, she was so intent.

Ryan asked, "You think maybe you can handle the other two on your own?"

"Of course."

"We got you covered here." Berto's crew members were jolly and seemingly tireless. "Your deputy can ride with us. Go save the world."

She was already moving for the car. "I'll call once this new issue has been sorted. If I can, I'll meet you at the final stop."

Ethan watched her punch the motor and spew gravel in her departure. She hit the siren and lights as she reached the drive's end. He was still standing there long after the wail faded into the night.

"You okay there, man?"

Ethan faced the driver, a burly African-American man named Jerry, who for once was not grinning. Ethan said, "I was thinking about her son. What it must mean, watching his mother leave to cover an emergency."

Jerry walked over to stand beside Ethan. "My uncle was a cop. His wife, my mom's sister, was after him to quit. The guy always told her the same thing. Some people are born to run toward trouble." The driver pointed to where his mate was closing the front door. "We're all done here. Who's next on your list?"

Six and a half hours later, the three of them finished loading the final home's artwork and the safe's contents. Dawn was a bleak affair, as if the fire's forces made battle with the sunrise. The blue sky and the high cirrus clouds and the faint light were all streaked and shadowed by smoke. The three of them—Ethan, Jerry, the driver, and Nate, his assistant—were silenced by weariness.

As they started to close the truck's rear doors,

Ethan spotted the newcomers. "Hold up there."

The animals, two dogs and a scrawny kitten, looked like gray figurines. Scarcely alive, their movements trembling and uncertain. Ash so caked their pelts it was impossible to tell what color they might once have been.

Nate handed down the portable hand pump with shower attachment. Ethan filled a water bowl, then opened the sack of feed and hand-fed the cat and one dog, while Jerry washed gunk off their pelts. The animals' flanks trembled constantly. Another handful of feed, then Ethan lifted the dog and settled him into the first plastic cage. He suspected it was a setter mix, and the cage made for a tight fit. But the dog scarcely seemed to notice.

The three men were almost as filthy as the animals by the time the smaller dog and then the cat were caged and the containers settled behind the truck's seat. That was when the fourth animal appeared.

Jerry muttered, "What on earth . . ."

The animal was smaller than the dogs, less than knee high, legs trembling.

Nate asked, "Is that . . ."

The animal bleated.

"A baby goat," Ethan realized. "Probably a miniature. Hand me the water bowl."

The day was taking full gray form by the time they arrived back at the town limits. Despite his exhaustion, Ethan found a genuine pleasure in rolling down his window and waving as they passed the street-side Santa.

They stopped by the vet's first, getting Piper out of bed. She was no more cross than usual, and seemed genuinely delighted with her new charges. From there, they went straight to the bank, driving along whisper-quiet streets and arriving while the night guard was still on duty. They unloaded the truck in no time flat. Ethan applied strips of masking tape to the cellar floor, marking boundaries, then used a felt-tip pen to write each family's name on the taped perimeters. He arrived home just as the sun peeked over the eastern tree line, and was asleep fifteen minutes later.

Ryan never called.

24

Ryan woke to a blade of afternoon sunlight tracing its way across her face. She knew it was afternoon because her bedroom window faced straight west. She lay there a moment, listening carefully. Ever since the last straggling rainfall ended and the desert blows began, afternoon sunlight meant the night would be a long one. Desert winds strengthened with the waning day and reached their peak around midnight, as if they knew when the frontline troops were at their weakest. But by midafternoon on such days, the wind moaned and blasted, flicking cinders and danger high into the cloudless sky.

But all she heard were voices.

Two of them.

This was hardly a surprise. Amara, her neighbor and friend and sitter, liked to keep Liam here in his home. The only time Amara brought Ryan's son to her house was when she fed the boy and her husband, Hakim, together. Otherwise, Liam stayed where he was happiest. And Amara found nothing whatsoever troubling about Liam's habitual silence. As Hakim liked to say, Amara could be happy talking to an empty room. As far as Ryan was concerned, Amara was a gift from above.

Only today Ryan did not hear Amara. The two voices she heard were both male.

She rose and dressed in clean LAPD sweats and started down the hall, only to be halted by the sound of her son saying, "So Avariel ran away."

"In a way. But not really. Not like he ran and stayed away. Avariel discovered what his father was planning, razing the forest around his grandmother's home."

"Building big houses."

"Exactly. And making that discovery broke the link between Avariel and the world his parents adored, the city and everything it meant. He stopped going to school. He rose before anyone else, stole food for the day, and left. They punished him, of course, and they tried to lock him up. But he found ways to escape. In the months leading up to Christmas, he left almost every day and went to the old house."

"And the forest."

"Of course the forest. But it was while exploring the house that he discovered his great-great-grandmother's diary. And learned he was one-sixteenth elf. And that the crystal pipe was kind of like a doorbell. It didn't open the way to the elven kingdom. It *asked*. The heart had to be true, and the reason had to be real . . ."

Ryan stepped into the main room, and found Ethan seated at the dining table, drawing pad open in front of him. Her son was sprawled on the living-room floor. He worked on another pad, pens and pencils scattered like a plastic rainbow around him.

Ethan smiled and said, "Hi, lovely lady."

Liam slapped his pad shut and jumped to his feet. "Finally."

Ethan turned to Liam. "Good morning, Mom. I hope you slept well."

"But it's afternoon."

Ethan just stared at the child. Finally Liam repeated the words. He used his worst toneless drone. But still.

Ethan said, "Good man."

Ryan kissed her son, ruffled his hair, and asked, "What did I miss?"

Liam announced, "Ethan brought us a tree."

"Correction. I have purchased a tree. I notice you don't have one. So if you like, I would be happy to make it a Christmas gift."

"Spoken like a banker." Ryan drifted over to the counter. Kissed Ethan. Ruffled his hair. Saw gray scattered in the dark, like he still carried a few flecks of ash. Was somehow touched by this sign of the passing years.

"I don't want to overstep my boundaries."

She was tempted to tell him it was far too late to worry about such things. But her son was watching them, standing by his pad, solemn and motionless. So she said, "Thank you, Mister Banker, sir. That is a most thoughtful gift."

She made coffee and watched through the window as her son and this new man in her life went outside and untied the tree strapped to the roof of his rental car. Liam carried the stand, and Ethan the tree, up the stairs and into her world.

Ryan located the boxes of lights and ornaments, stored last January at the back of the hall closet. Buried under shoes and bags of clothes Liam had outgrown, things she had meant for weeks to take down to the fire station. She sat on the counter and watched them string the lights and hang the decorations.

Ryan was about to rise and make herself breakfast when her son said, "I don't get it."

"What's that?"

"How Avariel found the chest."

"Ah. That marked the moment I fell in love with those stories. I still remember the first time I read that passage. It was like . . ."

Liam finished rimming the lower branches with tinsel. "What?"

"Like I had come home. Finally, at long last. I knew I belonged somewhere."

The room went quiet again. Ethan opened another box of lights. Liam hung a couple of baubles. Ryan needed another cup of coffee. She needed the bathroom. She needed to start her day. But nothing, not a single solitary thing, could possibly draw her away from her position on that kitchen stool. Waiting through the quiet moment. Waiting to hear what came next.

Finally Ethan said, "The question isn't how Avariel found the chest. The real issue is, how did he come to be in his grandmother's house at all. Remember, the reason he came to the estate was—"

"The forest."

"Exactly. So, why did he go inside? Why even bother? Avariel hated his home in the apartment building. What drew him into another house, one that held nothing but memories of the dead woman?"

As Ryan sat and watched her two men, a gold-feathered blur popped out of the bowl by Liam's sketch pad, flew over, stopped in midair, gave Ryan a careful inspection, then flitted back to the bowl. She heard her son say, "So . . ."

Ethan, she realized, was breaking up the story in order to draw Liam out. Make him comfortable with speaking.

There was no reason why the concept should make her eyes burn so. None whatsoever.

Ethan replied, "Avariel followed a ghost. Or so he thought. You see, elves are only real inside the forest. When they leave the glen, they become translucent. You know what that word means? No? The elves gradually lost their substance. The farther they moved away from the trees that made up their natural home, the less real they became.

So by the time the elf arrived at the house, he was little more than an idea. Just a trace of him was left. And it wasn't until much later that Avariel realized what a sacrifice the elf was making . . ."

Another long pause, until Liam finally offered, "For him."

"For the elven realm's very existence. See, they already knew their forest home was under threat. They needed a human to help them survive. Maybe."

Ryan waited with the man, until her beautiful son said, "So the elf . . ."

"The elf almost went too far. Which was why Avariel just saw a ghost. Any farther, just a few inches, and the elf would become fully erased."

"You mean . . . die?"

"Yes. Elves don't count time as we do. For them, centuries come and go, just like the ages of our oldest trees. So for the herald to move that far, to try and point Avariel toward the house and the chest and the diary, risked ending a life that had continued for years beyond count."

Ryan counted a dozen breaths, before she heard a soft, "Wow."

"Yes. But there's more."

She waited with Ethan for her son to say, "Tell me."

"The elf's name was Derion. He was the king's own messenger. He volunteered for this very dangerous mission because Derion was brother to Avariel's grandmother's grandmother. He had grieved all these years over how she had sacrificed her long elven life out of love for a human. And he had remained both furious and hurt over the loss. Only now there was this worthy child as a result, a young boy who loved the forest more than anything. A part-elven child who might—just might—save them all." Ethan was the one who went quiet. Then, "Derion was certain Avariel would see him and fight against the natural fear anyone might have of a ghost. And trust his heart. And go inside. And find the diary."

Liam finished, "And go home."

Ryan decided she had heard all one heart could bear. She cleared her face, rose from the stool, and entered the corridor she could scarcely see.

25

Miramar's oldest guesthouse was also the only one in the town center. All the others were strung like weather-beaten pearls along the ocean road. The century-old whitewashed house backed into a paved courtyard framed by a dozen studio apartments.

Ethan's phone rang as he approached the courtyard entrance. Ryan said, "I'm not going to make the party. Sorry. Work."

He heard the tension in her voice and tried to make light of it. "We will all miss you terribly."

"Liar."

"All the zing just went out of the night." He was only half joking. "Like a balloon—"

He was cut off by a loud squawk over Ryan's radio. She said, "Hang on, Ethan." A click, then, "Go ahead, Porter."

Ethan could not make out Porter's words. But the chief clearly shared Ryan's strain. Ethan recalled the previous night, seeing Ryan's features go drum-taut from yet another emergency call-out. He was almost ready when Ryan came back on, saying, "I have to go."

"Stay safe . . ." But she had already cut the connection. Ethan stowed his phone and entered the party.

The courtyard parking lot and the small garden rimming the pool now held a festive air. A parked ER vehicle had been done up with cardboard and paint and crepe paper and lights, and now saw duty as Santa's motorized sleigh. Christmas trees flanked long trestle tables holding an astonishing array of food and drinks. Loudspeakers strung from the lampposts played carols and swing-era holiday classics.

He stood there on the outskirts of the jolly crowd and watched as locals gave what they could, when they were able. No thanks expected or really even wanted. They didn't broadcast their deeds. Their gifts were made in the matter-of-fact way that made it Christmas, California style.

Dolores noticed him standing there on the perimeter and marched over. She planted fists on hips, just like she was about to lay into a teller who wasn't measuring up. "What is this? Mister Indemented is waiting for an engraved invitation?"

"*Indemented* isn't a word, and you know it."

"I'll give you all the words you can handle and more, you don't come over and lend us a hand." She jammed a peaked red hat on his head, grabbed his elbow, and tugged. "It's all hands on deck. Even Mister Indiscreet needs to take his place in line."

As she led him behind the central table, another bus pulled up and disgorged a weary yet jolly crew, their hair still wet from the showers, their gazes fractured by the strain of frontline duty.

Ethan became their designated turkey carver. There was also a side of barbecued beef, piles of roasted vegetables, mashed potatoes, and pumpkin pie—the works. And booze. Their guests might set a town record for knocking it back. But it was done with a fair semblance of order, especially with crew leaders, spouses, and assistant chiefs keeping a tight watch.

Twice an hour, the music paused for an extended weather update. Each time, everyone froze. Even the most rowdy were completely silenced. The predictions were dire. Strong desert winds expected within the next twenty-four to thirty-six hours.

Eventually Carl Reese, Ethan's boss, took over the carving knife and told him to take a break. Ethan filled a plate and walked over to where the lone female assistant chief was seated. "Mind some company?"

Ethan had never actually spoken with Maya, but he liked how she and Ryan had interacted on the line. Two confident women, both comfortable with crises and leadership.

She slid over, making room. "You're the new deputy. Do I have that right?"

"Just temporary."

"Sure. Like most of my crew. Glad you're helping out."

He waited until she finished her meal, then asked, "Is there any chance we could have a word?"

"What is it you think we're doing now?"

Ethan set down his fork. He could eat anytime. "A private word."

She led him over to where the bus idled, partially blocking the crowd from view. Maya made a point of checking her watch. "We're all due back on the fire line very soon."

"This won't take long." Swift as he could, Ethan sketched out what he knew about the two robberies, the missing caretaker, the frustrated and worried Belgian attorney, how they were stymied.

By the time Ethan detailed their meeting with Porter, the chief's attention was laser focused. "You share Ryan's suspicions the fires were deliberately set?"

"I'm more focused on the thefts. And the caretaker. And these second-generation owners."

"Who've blocked you from getting on their properties."

"Right."

"Does Ryan know we're talking?"

"Not yet. I wanted to see if you thought my idea had merit. If not, there's no reason to add something more to her day."

"Makes sense," Maya replied. "Want to tell me your big idea?"

"Yes."

Midway through, Maya crossed her arms and

began studying the pavement at her feet. She remained like that after he was done. "I need to run this by my boss."

"You think it might work?"

"What I think is, I need to run it by the boss. And so do you."

"Can't tonight. She's off putting out a different kind of fire. I'll speak with Ryan tomorrow, soon as she wakes up."

Maya took her time inspecting him. "Ryan tells me you lost your home to the blaze."

"Lost everything I owned, pretty much."

"So you've got some skin in this game."

"Is that a problem?"

Maya bobbed her head, clearly undecided. "Have Ryan call me when she's ready."

The forecast was mostly why the last crews filed meekly back into the waiting bus. Ethan helped clean up, then walked home. He had never imagined he might know such simple joy, being part of something greater. Allowing the spirit of Christmas to take hold in his heart. He was letting go, both of the emotional remnants of his failed marriage and the cocoon of safety.

When he climbed into bed, the clock read half past two. He counted it a good day indeed.

Ethan woke around midmorning. He should have slept longer, certainly his body ached for more rest. But his mind was already running at full speed.

While he made coffee, he watched the morning weather report. Or tried. Three minutes was all he could stand. The predictions were dire. And the sunlight streaming through his kitchen window seemed to defy what he was hearing. The trees were still, the sky dappled with lazy clouds. He opened his door to a wintry chill and stood there, wondering how long he should wait before calling Ryan.

He decided to text, saying there was something he needed to speak with her about. And could he spend some time with Liam. Even before finishing the text, he was planning their day together.

He returned to the kitchen only long enough to recharge his mug and prepare a breakfast of yogurt and berries and a topping of granola. While he ate, Ethan scrolled through his emails. Four more absentee families asked to have their valuables placed in the bank. The emails had gone from cautious to near panic. Clearly, they had been spooked by the same weather warnings.

There was still nothing from the Belgian attorney.

As Ethan spoke with Jerry, the driver, arranging for them to head out that afternoon, Ryan texted and asked him to come over.

Ryan emerged from her bedroom just before noon. Amara, bless her, took one look at Ryan's face and ushered Liam from the apartment. She had gone to bed with her nerves still taut from a very hard night—a break-in at one of Miramar's upscale shops, followed by a domestic dispute. Family interventions were among Ryan's worst duties, partly because they were so hard for her to shake off. She had slept poorly and twice woken from dreams she could not recall, other than the acrid echo of angry voices.

Forty-five minutes later, she was dressed and standing by her kitchen window when Ethan pulled up. A guy she had personally deputized was coming over to discuss an idea he'd had. One that Maya Ricardo, the assistant fire chief, had texted her about, saying it might have potential. Nothing more. Ethan rose from the car and searched the building's windows. He spotted Ryan standing there and smiled and waved. Ryan felt the previous night's strain weigh down her limbs, making it a genuine struggle to wave in response.

He entered the apartment, asked about Liam, accepted a mug. The day was mild enough for them to go back outside and sit on the building's front steps. Ryan studied a dark ribbon of smoke in the otherwise very blue morning sky and listened as he outlined his idea.

When she looked back, it seemed as though every word Ethan spoke ratcheted up her internal tension. The previous night's issues raised their venomous head, threatening to strike her anew with the poison of helpless heartache. She leaned away from him, pretending to listen, but now his words were filtered through rage and arguments and bitter regret—both last night's, and the ashes of her own futile struggle from long ago.

After Ethan stopped talking, she let the silence build. Ryan watched a trio of ravens fly back and forth above the parking lot. Their wings moved in slow sweeps, as if they, too, had to fight their way through a tide of cold regret.

Ethan's idea was fairly good, as ideas went. But there were any number of issues that made it borderline illegal. She knew what Porter would say. Elements of the plan threatened to pull them in the wrong direction. Porter was a by-the-book sort of police officer. Which was one reason Ryan loved working with him. One of many.

And then there was the other thing: the shroud that had draped itself over the day.

Ethan cleared his throat. He had been made uncommonly nervous by her silence. "Is something the matter?"

"Why are you doing this?" She heard the edge to her voice. The cop-on-duty tone. And she knew there was nothing she could do about it. "Because you've lost everything?"

Ethan cleared his throat a second time. "Maya asked me the same thing. Sort of. What she said was, I had skin in the game. I asked if that was a problem. It seemed to me like she wasn't sure how to respond."

"She's a frontline officer. Just like me." Ryan felt the tension build, strong as a concrete barrier between them. "If this is a revenge thing, I need to know. Revenge might work in the movies. But it makes for a dangerous state in real police work. Acting on revenge can get innocent people hurt."

"I understand that."

"So answer the question."

Ethan's jaw muscles worked, like he needed to chew on the thoughts. His voice remained steady, but there was a spark to his gaze now. It was an anger she hadn't seen before. "I can't deny it. Revenge definitely plays a part."

"Then the answer is no." She heard the same cold-iron tone she had used the previous night. Knew it was angering him. Knew also there was nothing she could do about it. "Whether or not we act on your suggestion, you can't be a part of it."

"Ryan . . ."

"What?"

"Okay, I understand your concern. But revenge is not the dominant factor here."

"I can't take that risk."

"Ryan, listen to me. I want to catch the bad guys. I want to arrest them. Yes, I want to know if they had a hand in setting the fires that cost me everything. But I accept we'll probably never be certain." His anger was stronger now, almost making a lie of his calm tone. "Isn't that enough?"

"Enough for what?" She felt incapable of pulling back. Stop using the cop voice with him. Seated here on her front steps, the man who had gone from being a deputized civilian to someone who genuinely cared for her. And for her son. Not forgetting that for an instant. Even so, just then it was the police detective who responded. "You were deputized for a specific duty. Help retrieve valuables from homes damaged by the fire. This was expanded to include homes under threat. Store the items safely in your bank until the situation stabilized. What you're asking to be a part of is—"

"Is what? Wrong?"

"I was going to say, part of regular police action. But yes, Ethan. *Wrong* works. You are not trained for this sort of duty. What you're suggesting carries a very real risk."

"Who are we risking, Ryan? I'm trying to save others from being robbed!"

"You're risking me. My professional standing. You risk having my police department enter into an illegal action."

"Illegal how?"

She nodded. "That's the issue. You don't have training in proper police tactics. For you, stepping over the line is not a problem, because you have no idea where the legal line is." She kept nodding, pushing back. Cold. Detached. "And then there is the revenge element. Because the risk is, in a heated situation, you may not care which side of the line you're walking. But I do. I have to. It's part of my job. As a *real* police officer. I am here to *uphold the law.*"

"I thought it was to protect and serve. Didn't I hear that somewhere?"

"Of course, Ethan. Yes. You did. And I do. Within the law."

"What about justice?"

"Justice is an issue for the courts. Not us. We are the front line. We are nothing if we don't have the law on our side." She probably should have stopped there. But she didn't. "My concern, the reason why we're talking about this at all, is because you're equating *justice* with *revenge.* Get the bad guys. Put them down. Regardless of which side of the legal line you wind up standing on. Tell me I'm wrong."

There was a flush to his features, a hard tight glint to his gaze. "You've got a strange way of thanking me for helping out."

"But this new idea of yours, Ethan, is *not* helping." There were a thousand things more she wanted to say. But a tiny sliver of control held her back, though at the moment she could not say why. The temptation to draw out all the old rage, open the cage of past regrets and let them fly, almost overwhelmed her. But not quite. She knew the only way to stay silent was to put some distance between her and this confrontation. "Now I need to go be a real cop."

Ethan rose to his feet with her. "That's it?"

She wheeled about. Armed and ready. "What else is there, Ethan?"

But he merely stood there, sullen and silent. Refusing to rise to the bait and argue. Which she wanted in a strange sort of way. Though it hurt. Though she knew a totally wrong instinct was at work, something drawn from her previous life. One that still stained her days.

Ryan slipped behind the wheel and started the engine. She could not help but glance back and see Ethan still standing there on her front step. As she put the car in drive, she knew it was the fear of being hurt again that pushed her away. All the reasons she had spent years building up, keeping men and love at a safe distance. She knew her anger had almost nothing to do with Ethan's idea, or his motives, or even this conversation. And she was helpless to do anything about it. Her shield against ever being left alone again, hurting and frightened, was too strong. It kept her safe.

26

Ryan parked beside the same horse trailer that had brought the mare and her foal from the barn. Recalling the events and how close she had been to Ethan that night left her feeling even worse.

As she rose from the car, Carol Wright emerged from the barn. She held an oversized nursing bottle and led the foal by a rope halter. "Just in time. Come give me a hand."

Ryan followed Carol into the barn's shadows, back to where the mare was stomping her hooves and trying to pull her head free of the side post where she was tied.

"Here's your baby, darling. Now just settle." Carol untied the mare and let her snuffle her foal. "The mama keeps trying to insert herself between me and the baby. Take hold of her collar. No, farther up, and stand so she can keep an eye on us." Carol squatted by the foal and offered her the bottle. "Piper thinks the little one needs some extra help putting on weight."

Ryan stroked the mare's neck. "I need to have a word with Porter."

"He's running on Christmas time. Still in the shower." Carol smiled as the foal pulled hard on

189

the bottle. "I want to name her Beauty, but Porter won't let me. Not yet, anyway. But my man has started getting that broody look every time he enters the barn. He'll come around."

Ryan felt the mare starting to shift toward Carol and pushed back. A gentle nudge was enough. And suddenly she found her eyes burning, the lump back in her throat. She settled her forehead on the horse's flank.

"Ryan, honey, what's wrong?"

She found it easier to talk with her eyes closed and her face pressed against the mare. Surrounded by the fragrances of straw and horse and leather. She described hearing Ethan's idea, without actually telling Carol what it was, then finished, "I responded like a cop. Hard as nails. I could hear it, and didn't seem able to change how . . ." She sighed. "I feel just awful."

"All right, Beauty. We're done now. Go on back to mama." Carol released the foal and settled against a corral post. "You sound just like Porter. He comes in after a bad shift, and the things he's been through are still on him like a bad stench."

Ryan released the mare and breathed around the truth. Or tried to. "I had a rough night."

"Porter told me. Not what it was. Just that it had turned hard on you both."

"I couldn't let it go. Sitting there with Ethan, I couldn't . . ."

"The hours you people have been working, the strain of this fire on top of all the town's other problems, I doubt you're ever really off duty."

Ryan found herself thinking back to earlier days. "My ex had a lot of Peter Pan in him. You know what I mean."

"Of course I do."

"He loved nothing more than roaming through nights with his engine at redline. The 'skyrocket life' was how he put it. And for a while, I loved it too. But I wanted to grow up. Have a family. Start a career. He saw nothing ahead of him but chains."

"And then came Liam." Carol set the empty bottle down beside her. "And the man you loved ran away."

"For the longest time, that's all I saw. My ex ran away from his son and everything having a child meant. But the truth is actually more complicated."

"It often is."

"I was the one who abandoned the life he wanted."

"You grew up. He didn't." Carol patted the stable floor. "Come sit with me." As Ryan settled, she went on, "And then along comes Ethan."

"Ethan is such a good sweet man. He's great with Liam. And I . . ."

"You're in love."

The words were softly spoken, yet they struck

Ryan with the force of a mallet applied directly at heart level.

"You're a cop. And you're in love. And sometimes the two things are going to be at direct odds with each other. And yes, that means you're going to talk and act like you're still on the job. With a man who deserves better."

Ryan jammed the palms of her hands on her eyes. She pressed as hard as she could. Clenched up tight. Pushing the shame and heat back inside. Where it all belonged. "I'm so scared."

"Of being in love? Or getting things wrong?"

"Both. You know it's both."

"Of course I do. And so do you." Carol patted her shoulder. Stroked her, like she had the foal. "You're a good person. And you're aware. You're going into this with your eyes open. Did you apologize?"

"Not yet. I just couldn't . . ."

"Let go of the past."

Having Carol understand her so well almost robbed Ryan of control. "I feel like ten kinds of fool."

"When you're ready, tell him you're sorry. Knowing Ethan, my guess is, he's already in the process of forgiving and moving on."

In the distance, a door slammed. "Carol?"

"In here." Carol rose to her feet, then offered Ryan her hand. "You need a minute?"

"No." She wiped her face. "I'm good."

Carol draped an arm around her shoulder and led her into the daylight. "You most certainly are."

As Ryan recounted Ethan's concept, Porter only moved once, when he rose from his desk, crossed the office, shut the door, and then resumed his seat. "Go on," he said.

When she was finished, he sat staring at the window, frowning in concentration. Ryan was more than content to wait with him. Even though she hated how the silence gave her ample room to fret.

She could not remember how she'd been before Liam was born, but she wanted to believe that her present normal comfort with quiet hours had always been there. Not as strong as now. But still was present. A component of who she had always been at some level.

Her ex was the loud one. He had always loved hearing the sound of his own full-throated roar. Wild nights of running—that line from the Don Henley song "Everything Is Different Now" had once been his trademark. Maybe it still was, for all she knew. But her ex had never accepted the song's next line, how a starving soul could only live like that for so long.

A starving soul. The words pulsed deep in the room's quiet. There were all kinds of hungry spirits. Maybe that was why her anger with Ethan

193

still lingered. Down deep, at a level where her logic could not reach, down in her bones and her heart, she had no choice but to admit that one big reason for her anger was that Ethan had made her realize just how famished her heart had become.

Thankfully, Porter chose that moment to break the silence. "What did you tell Ethan?"

"I said revenge didn't work as a motive for a cop. And because of that, if we ever decided to move on this, he couldn't be a part of the action." She hesitated, then added, "I was tough on the guy, how I reacted. He deserved better."

"How did he take it?"

"Not well."

"But he understands?"

She shook her head. "Sometimes that man is as hard to read as my son."

Porter sipped from his mug. "You heard the latest?"

Ryan knew he meant the weather. "Much as I could bear."

"Doesn't look good."

"No. It doesn't."

"Could be a long night." Porter rose and walked to the window. Staring at the town beyond the station's perimeter fence. "Sheriff's office has asked for a liaison to help with their patrols. I want you to handle it. Let Ethan work with Berto's truck on clearing the houses well removed from the danger zone."

"Makes sense." She tested her internal state, like she would the air. Wondering how she felt. Deciding it was a good thing, working a night shift well removed from Ethan. But it was painful just the same. "What do you think of the idea?"

"I had been up half the night worrying about it, you know," he answered.

"The perps possibly hiding behind estate walls and a barred gate."

"Not to mention being shielded by a lawyer seven thousand miles away."

"But we don't know anything. Not for certain," she stated.

Porter nodded to the day. "Still. It eats at me."

She released the worry. "Was I wrong to put Ethan down?"

"No." Definite. "The man doesn't know procedure. His involvement could result in evidence we can't use in court. Not to mention how one false move might have us all standing on the wrong side of the law."

She wanted to ask why being right still left her feeling so awful. But there was nothing to be gained in that. Ryan rose from her chair. "I better reach out to the sheriff."

Porter was still standing there, studying the day, when she left.

27

Ethan returned home, changed into his fire-stained clothes, and left for another shift. He met the construction company's truck and Berto's two trusted employees at the bank, where they spent a couple of hours shifting the goods already retrieved into tighter spaces, then marking out more squares with masking tape, readying for the next load.

Ethan unfolded the page holding the new list of homes, and together they planned out the night's schedule. As they drove out of town, Ethan decided there was no need to call Ryan with an update. If she wanted to know, she had his number.

Wishing it was easier to keep his phone in his pocket. Wishing it was easier to enter the night without her.

They needed the better part of six hours to work their way through the new list. Ethan's mind remained fastened on a grim litany, replaying the argument and all the reasons why Ryan was wrong to have responded as she had. The driver, Jerry, and his assistant caught wind of Ethan's internal state and worked in utter silence—avoiding his gaze, keeping their distance wherever possible.

The only glimmer of goodness was that the wind never arrived. The night stayed clear and cold, their work proceeded smoothly. Not a single animal appeared.

They stowed their load in the bank's cellar, sealed the makeshift safe, bade each other a quiet good night, and Ethan was left alone with his unsettled heart.

He woke just before midday, as usual to the faint hint of smoke and the soft hum of unseen wings.

Only this time, when he opened his eyes, Ethan realized he was still dreaming.

Or at least he desperately hoped so.

He stood in the middle of a fire-ravaged town. The remnants of what once had been Miramar rose around him like broken teeth. Gray ash covered the earth and drifted in morose eddies, like tears once shed and now forgotten.

Then he truly woke, his heart pounding, lungs gasping for a breath of clean air.

As he rose from his bed, Ethan was frozen in place by a question. Or by doubt. Or by a fearful new reality. What if the image was of a love now lost?

He left his home nine minutes later. Rushing now. Desperate to heal the rift. Neither blame nor accountability mattered. Not when facing the ruins of what might have been.

When he pulled up in front of Ryan's building, Ethan had not worked out precisely what he was going to say. He sat in his car, staring at the empty window, hoping for inspiration.

Amara stepped from the neighboring building, spotted him, and rushed over. As Ethan rose from the car, she greeted him with, "The lady is still asleep. I was just going to make the little one lunch."

It was good, Ethan reflected, to see both acceptance and approval in the woman's gaze. Or so he hoped.

"Do you think it would be okay if I took him somewhere?"

"The lady's two men off together? I think it would be wonderful, and so would Ryan." Her dark eyes sparkled with a light as sweet as her accent, which Ethan could not place. "You do the two of them much good, Mr. Lange."

"Please. Call me Ethan."

"Ryan is too much alone. She has spent too many nights wishing for a man like you." She patted his arm and started away. "Don't you dare tell her I said that."

Ethan entered the apartment to find Liam in his customary position, partially hidden by the Christmas tree, the flickering lights forming liquid images on his sketch pad. Trevor was propped on the side of his bowl, studying the boy. Soon as Ethan stepped inside, Liam closed the pad, gathered his pens, and rose. "Finally."

Ethan tried to tell himself it was silly to feel that good over the boy's one-word greeting. He offered Liam a brief hug, and was made happier still by how the boy responded by wrapping the hand not holding his artwork around Ethan's waist.

"How's my little man?"

"Hungry."

"Hungry is good. Let me hang this, and we'll head out." Ethan searched the kitchen area, and settled on a ceiling hook above the side counter. He took down the copper pan and in its place hung the hummingbird feeder he had taken from his own front porch. "I think we need to accept that Trevor is here to stay. Which means he needs to learn how to feed for himself when you're not around. When is his next meal?"

Liam pulled his phone from his pocket. "Fifteen minutes."

"Feed him now. Then we leave him here today. When we get back, we'll see if he managed to find the new food. If he didn't, we will hopefully get back before Trevor grows too hungry."

In response, Liam went back for the bowl, set it on the counter, plied the dropper, then announced, "Ready."

Ethan used the phone pad and wrote Ryan a note. He started to apologize in writing, but decided it was an easy out. So he closed after promising to bring her lunch. "We can go wherever you like. What are you in the mood for?"

"Anything?"

"Today's lunch is your call."

Liam headed for the door. "Tacos."

Ryan woke to the sound of her front door clicking shut. The instant she padded into her front room and saw the slip of paper on her kitchen counter, she knew two things. Long before she read the words, she knew. First, her son was with Ethan. Second, Carol was right. Ethan was already putting the quarrel behind him.

As she put on coffee and headed back to her bedroom to get dressed, she decided that this was a time for celebration.

Standing with her back to the window, she ate a half bowl of granola. There was no way she could keep the wind and weather from impacting her day. But she resisted her urge to make her customary first check for bad news. As she washed the bowl, her phone chimed with a text from Ethan, saying they were eating tacos and asking if he could bring her lunch.

As she texted him back, she noticed the change to her kitchen.

A bird feeder was draped from the hook that had formerly held her copper-bottom cooking pot. A string of tinsel was wrapped around the cord. As she watched, Trevor flashed into view, hovered by the feeder, drank, and flew back to his bowl.

Ryan poured a fresh coffee into her go-cup and headed out.

Miramar's main bookshop was midway down the central shopping avenue. The family who ran the shop also owned the building, and as more customers had shifted to ebooks they had sold their home, moved into the upstairs apartment, expanded their inventory, and managed to stay afloat. Barely. Nowadays they sold gifts, seasonal wares, clothes, whatever drew the clientele. On night patrol several weeks earlier, Ryan had spied a new item displayed in their window. The hooded sweatshirt had an elf on its front, only this one wore a Mohawk haircut and wraparound shades. The elf's neck and shaved head were heavily tattooed. His inked arms were crossed over a leather vest with a chest patch reading BORN TO RIDE. The lace-up boots had metal tips. Matching metal rimmed his tall ears. The elf leaned against a Harley lowrider. CHRISTMAS RULES was written beneath the image.

Viola Calais, co-owner, was behind the counter. "Look who the cat dragged in."

"My son will totally love that awful thing you have in your window, I'm sorry to say."

"How old is he now?"

"A small eleven."

"I think we've sold out of smaller sizes, but I'll check. Mind the shop, will you? I'm all by myself."

"No problem."

"It's amazing how many semi-disgusted parents we've had come in to buy that."

"You don't like it either?"

"Hon, anything that brings in this many buyers is fine in my book." She headed toward the back. "Bad joke."

While Ryan stood sentry, she noticed the three rows of books behind the register. She slipped around the counter, pulled one down at random, saw the price, and gasped.

Viola returned carrying a sweatshirt. "This is the smallest we have left. It will probably be a tad too large, but he'll grow."

"Lucky me." Ryan held up the book. "Nine hundred dollars? Really?"

"Those are my husband's pride and joy." Viola took the book and slipped it back into place. "Ford has collected rare books his entire life. And for your information, that price is a solid deal. Values are generally set online nowadays. Ford used to only let go of his duplicates. Now we're up for anything that brings us a sale. Those little gems kept us afloat during the recent downturn." Viola unfolded the sweatshirt and spread it on the counter. "What do you think?"

"It looks even more horrid close-up than it did in the window."

"Hon, I'm talking about the size."

"You're right. It's too big. But I doubt Liam will mind even a little bit."

"I assume we want this gift wrapped."

"Yes, please . . . Have you ever heard of the Elven Child series?"

Viola looked up. "Not you too."

"Excuse me?"

"Ethan Lange has a standing order . . ." She paused. Did her best to smother her smile. "Oh. I see."

Ryan felt her face flame. "I'm just asking."

"Of course you were, hon." Viola tore off a sheet of wrapping paper. "How is the dear deputy?"

"You can just stow that smugness in your back pocket where it belongs."

"To answer your question, Ford has managed to locate a copy of the first volume, the title—"

"*The Crystal Pipe*."

"The condition is nowhere near what the seller claimed. The cover is bent, and several pages are stained. Which is why we never told Ethan it had come in. Ford is sending it back."

"Can I see it?"

Viola cast her a knowing glance. But all she said was "Just a minute."

Viola took much longer this time. When she

finally returned from upstairs, she said, "The best thing I can say about it is, all the pages are intact."

The book was in fairly dreadful shape. "How much?"

Viola nodded. "Ford just got off the phone with the seller. They settled on fifty dollars. A volume in pristine shape will be five times that."

Ryan set her card on the counter. "Wrap that up too, please."

28

Ethan's first stop was the strip mall near Piper's practice. The taqueria specialized in slow-cooked meats, rendered soft and velvety, and served in a piquant sauce of their own making. Ethan ordered three beef tacos, three chicken, and double portions of ink-dark beans and Mexican slaw. He laughed at Liam's evident pleasure at everything. The only thing that would have made the hour finer would be sharing it with a woman who could be warm as the sun, and cold as frozen iron, all in the space of two breaths. As Ethan plied a trio of napkins, trying to clear the boy's face of the meal's remnants, he was struck by the reality there in front of him, in the pale face and trusting eyes. Here was what it meant to be a cop. The front line, she had called it. The memory carried a lance of very real pain, one he saw there in Liam's steady gaze.

He had once heard a woman's emotions described as tides called by the moon. But that wasn't true in Ryan's case. Hers were more like the blur of a hummingbird's wings. They shifted fast because they had to. From a loving mother to the defender of her people, her town, her laws. And then back.

As they drove the short distance to the vet's office, Liam asked, "Are you working with Mom again tonight?"

"Depends on her schedule. I'm definitely going out. We have several more houses to pack up and shift into the bank. Did your mom tell you about that?"

He nodded. "I get scared when she goes."

"I expect you do."

His words frosted the side window. "Especially at night."

Ethan had no idea how to respond, except to reach over for the boy's hand.

The rescued animals were resting calmly in the pens behind the vet's practice. Piper's assistant groomer was a young woman scarcely out of her teens, who took genuine pleasure in describing the trouble she'd had getting ash out of the goat's pelt. The miniature beast was settled in fresh straw, with the cat nestled up to her chin. The two dogs were both English spaniels, and fought one another for Liam's attention.

Piper came out while Liam was stroking the pygmy goat. "How's my favorite bird?"

Liam switched his attention to the cat. "Trevor still won't leave."

The vet squatted down beside him. "Does he fly?"

"Some. Not a lot."

"His lungs may have been damaged by the

smoke. How would you feel about keeping him for good?"

Liam continued stroking the cat. "He needs a friend."

Piper cast Ethan a look deep with affection. "You know all about that, don't you."

Liam's phone chimed. The boy said, "It's time to feed Trevor."

Ethan offered Piper a swift embrace, surprising them both. "I guess we better head out."

It was then, as they returned to the car, that Ethan realized he was in love.

Driving back to the apartment, Ethan could look back over its gradual unfolding. It was only now, though, that he could see it for what it had become. Not just the growing affection. The cost.

It was up to him to decide. Could he be man enough to accept the raw and rough with the good? Could he help her recover from the dark hours, the things she would never speak of? Even when they continued to stain her gaze long after the shift was over and she returned to them?

29

R yan was on the phone with Porter when Ethan's car pulled into the lot. She tried to pay attention to what the chief was telling her, and failed. She felt almost giddy at the sight of Ethan and Liam rising from his rental, a gray Chevy that matched the overcast day. The two of them smiled in a way that defied the grim light. As if they were capable of bringing their own warmth into this chill afternoon. "Porter, I have to go."

"So you'll speak with Ethan about this?"

"He just pulled up."

"You need to be ready to move soon as we get the call."

"You got it." She cut the connection and stood there, uncertain what to do. What she wanted was to cross the room, open the door, and fling herself into his arms. But just then any movement was simply beyond her.

Ethan, however, showed no such hesitation. He followed Liam into the apartment, set her meal on the counter, and seemed to levitate across the kitchen. "I'm so sorry, I—"

That was as far as she let him get. Ryan wrapped her arms around him, kissed him, pulled back far enough to search his face, and then found the silent assurance she needed that the bad moment was behind them. And kissed him again.

Then another pair of arms enveloped them at waist level, one arm around Ryan, the other around him, and a head inserted itself between them. Not wedging them apart. Nestling. Being a part of this incredible moment.

Ryan was still searching for the right words, something fine and big enough to fit around the sensation of these two men holding her. Abruptly Liam broke free. "Trevor is eating from the feeder."

"Right." Ethan continued to hold her close, his face nestled in her hair. "Good."

Liam bounded from the room. His abrupt departure was enough for the two of them to take a half-step back. Ethan asked, "Was it something I said?"

She kept a firm hold of both his hands. "Ethan . . ."

He pulled back a fraction more, as far as he could without releasing her. "There's a lot of truth in what you said. I didn't like hearing it. But that doesn't make it wrong."

"I'm so sorry," Ryan said.

"For what?"

"You know for what. There were a hundred ways I could have said it better. A thousand. And what did I do? I put on my cop face."

He did his best to smile. "It's a very pretty face."

"You're not going to let me apologize . . ."

"Ryan, you said it yourself. I'm just a temp working on things I don't understand."

She loved the warmth in his eyes, the feel of his arms. She could have stayed there all day. For months, in fact. But the call from her chief meant they were counting down precious moments. Far too few of them.

She was about to relate the chief's message, when Liam returned to the main room carrying his sketch pad. He knelt on the floor by their feet, lifted his gaze, and said, "Look."

Ethan released her and squatted down. Liam started on what he always did when showing Ryan his work. He flipped open the pad, gave Ethan maybe three seconds, then turned the page.

"Stop right there."

The sharp volume startled them both. Liam looked over, eyes round.

Ethan did not even glance at the boy. "Go back to the first page. All right. Move your hand. No, Liam, you can't turn the page until I tell you."

Ryan watched the man kneel and give Liam's work such total and complete attention it gave her chills. She did not want to disturb this moment. But she had to see. She quietly lifted a stool and moved it over to where she could seat herself and peer between them.

What she saw was shocking.

All Liam's art, at least those sketches she had managed to glimpse, followed the jagged electric quality of gaming videos and comics based on those games. This was similar, and yet totally different. A unique blend of electric, action-oriented figures and . . .

Ethan asked, "This is the palace?"

Liam nodded.

"Okay. Why do the walls bend like this?" When Liam remained silent, Ethan's voice sharpened. But it wasn't a bad thing. Just demanding. "Work with me, Liam."

"It's the tree."

"Of course. Yes. I see it now."

The palace was flanked by video-game-inspired fighters, with helmets and spears and boots and shields and long pointed ears. But the palace itself, the palace . . .

"Liam, this is amazing."

Amazing was the word. The palace *flowed*. It was a structure that wove its way up, bending and shifting . . .

Like a tree.

"Okay. Next one."

Ryan's phone chose that moment to chime. She checked the screen, saw it was Porter's alert. "Ethan . . ."

"Hold that thought." Ethan traced his finger above the bending, stretching, elongated house.

211

"You've designed this home to fit inside a branch?"

Liam nodded.

"Okay, next?" When the next page came into view, Ethan actually laughed. "A leaf home!"

"You said they could get smaller."

"Liam, this is . . ."

He noticed Ryan then, her expression, the way she held out the phone, like it was a warning she couldn't bring herself to actually say. Speak it and break the spell.

"What?" he asked.

Ryan said, "I discussed your concept with Porter. He and Maya have decided to go with it. Tonight, Ethan. They're doing it. I have to leave. You can come. But we have to move now."

"Three minutes." Ethan leaned back over the pad. "How many more?"

"Lots."

"Okay, we'll do a quick scan now, and then go over them in more detail later." He leaned in closer still, on all fours now, head within a foot of the pages, shifting back and forth as Liam turned. When the last page was done, he leaned back, sighed, and said, "Wow."

Liam actually laughed.

Ryan pressed, "Ethan . . ."

"Sure. Right." He seemed to have trouble getting to his feet. Looked down at her son. "Liam . . . wow!"

Liam leapt to his feet, rushed over, hugged the man.

It felt like the simplest thing in the world for Ryan to set down her phone and join in the moment. Holding them both. Allowing time to stand still. For a few quick breaths . . .

Almost long enough.

30

While she slipped into her uniform, Ryan asked Ethan to contact Amara. She texted Porter that they were on their way. Hugged her little man. As they hurried down the building's front stairs, she saw Ethan was holding the bag of food she had forgotten, and realized she was starving.

"Will you drive? I haven't eaten anything today except half a bowl of 'nola."

He flashed her mock round eyes. "Drive a real cop car? Are you serious?"

She tossed him the keys. "If you're a good little deputy, I might even let you turn on the lights and siren."

"Hold that thought." He slipped behind the wheel, started the motor, then asked, "Can I make a call on your phone?"

"Sure. Why not use yours?"

"Because I want you to hear this. Put it on the car speaker and turn up the volume." He gave her the number from memory. Then, "The next voice you hear will be Noah Hearst. He's one of the top set designers in Hollywood. Specializes in projects where there's a combination of CGI and real construction."

When the phone went to voice mail, Ethan said,

"Noah, it's Ethan. I'm using a friend's phone. Call me. I have news."

When she cut the connection, Ethan asked, "I suppose now is as good a time as any to ask where I'm supposed to be going."

"We're meeting at the station. Did your call have something to do with Liam's art?"

He slowed, turned, grinned, and said, "I thought you were hungry."

"Listen, bub. You're dealing with an armed officer of the law." Which was when her phone chimed. "It's your guy."

"Put him on speaker again." When the phone clicked, Ethan said, "Noah? You got a second?"

"I'm standing in a checkout line that's six miles long. Buying Christmas presents for my two nieces. I would pay good money for something to do."

"I completed my preliminary sketches a couple of days ago."

"Ethan, were you listening when I told you this was extremely urgent?"

"Absolutely."

"I've got old man Chambers and his sixteen assistants breathing down my collar. Why am I only hearing from you now?"

"Because."

"Oh. Well. That makes everything just hunky-dory, then. Hang on, I think I see a lipstick Taser in the display just up ahead."

"There's this young man I've been working with. His name is Liam."

"He's an artist?"

"Yes, Noah. He is. And he's been working on a series of concepts."

"For me?"

"Right."

"And?"

"I would happily toss my ideas into the garbage."

"Don't you dare. Really, Ethan? You're not just pulling my chain?"

"Remember what you said the first time we spoke. The challenge is how to make a story that's been out of print for over half a century live for a new generation. This is what he's done. My own work is . . ."

"Tell me."

"It's dated. It's based on images I've carried since my own childhood. His are based on the *now*."

A brief silence. "How old is this guy?"

"Eleven."

"Say again."

"He's eleven years old, and it doesn't matter. Well, it does, but not like you think. He just showed me his work. And it was . . ."

"I'm waiting."

"I felt like the stories that carried me through some really hard times were plucked from my own past, and brought right up to today."

"Okay. I confess. Chills."

"I can definitely base my models on his concepts. And something more. I think we can merge what he's designing into the larger CGI images. Not one or the other. Both together."

Another tight moment, then: "I don't want you sending these by courier. Not this close to Christmas. I'm talking with the Chambers exec in an hour. I'll see if they'll send a studio limo up tomorrow."

"Text me with instructions, Noah. We're heading out for another shift on the fire line."

"Same old, same old, right?" The man wasn't quite laughing. But close. "You just made my Christmas."

Ethan turned down the side street, pulled through the exterior fence, and parked in the police lot. He cut the motor, studied her a long moment, then said, "Ryan, I didn't mean to make you cry."

31

Six of them were crammed around one end of Porter's narrow conference table—Porter, Ryan, Maya, and Maya's assistant, Raj. The chief also asked Maud to join them, leaving the front office and phones unmanned. Ethan was seated beside Maud, his chair pushed slightly farther away from the table. As if he meant to show everyone that he was not really a part of what was about to happen.

Maybe.

A video screen was set up on the table's far end. Dirk Powell, the region's best-known weatherman, appeared on it.

Ryan heard him say, "I'm not entirely clear on what it is you're asking."

There was a surreal quality to Ryan's perspective. Everything was filtered through what she had heard in the police car. Ethan. Talking to the set designer. In Hollywood. About her son. And his sketches. She would remember every tiny fraction of that conversation for the rest of her life.

Somehow she still held the plastic bag containing the tacos she had not eaten. The fragrance of spicy chicken and chorizo was powerful, like incense. To her left, Ethan's face was partly hidden on Porter's other side. She could lean forward and see him. She wanted to, and yet there was no need. They were bound together, the policewoman and the artist-banker. And Liam. Not simply because he was Ryan's child. Ethan cared for her son. He *loved* the silent boy. He was *proud* of Liam.

She had shed silly tears in the car. Despite all the effort she could muster, she felt the urge to do so again. Here. In the police station.

Beyond absurd.

As Porter took his time introducing each of the people around the table, she clenched down harder still. He finished with Ethan, naming him simply as the town's newest deputy.

Dirk wore a chalk-blue dress shirt and matching silk tie. A cosmetician's napkin was tucked around his collar.

The weatherman's forehead had an oily sheen that highlighted his receding hairline. Dirk's trademark white-tooth smile was absent. When Porter went silent, he asked, "Am I in trouble?"

"Not with me. Absolutely not."

"I'm due again on air in twelve minutes."

"This won't take long. All we need is a fresh update on the weather."

"I know the past two days haven't met my predictions. And there's nothing I can do about it. And it's not just me. The National Weather Service is going nuts." He lifted his arms, revealing dark patches on his shirt. "There's this huge high over the western Rockies, a massive system that's growing bigger by the hour. But it's being held in check by a second smaller system off the coast. We've been expecting the Pacific system to dissolve for two days—"

He stopped when Porter held up one hand. Ryan couldn't be certain, but she suspected the chief was actually enjoying himself. "We know all that. What I want is your prediction for the next six to eight hours."

"I don't understand."

"Best guess. Nothing more."

"Exactly what I said on air half an hour ago. Zero chance of significant rainfall. Winds straight out of the west before dawn. Gusts tomorrow of fifty miles per hour. Maybe higher."

Maya and Raj shifted in their chairs, readying to spring into action. Porter glanced over. Five seconds. Less. The two people stilled.

He went back to the man on the screen. "I want you to push that forward a little."

"I'm sorry . . . What?"

Porter checked his watch. "It's just gone six. Sunset was, what . . ."

"An hour ago," Maya replied. "We're approaching full dark."

Porter asked, "Could the winds theoretically be arriving around, say, seven thirty?"

"You're serious."

Porter smiled. "Serious as an arrest warrant."

The weatherman grimaced like he'd just bitten down on a bad lemon.

"And one more thing. Start all your reports this evening with a red-alarm warning. Fire spreading to Tinnerman Ridge and . . ."

Ethan spoke for the first time. "Long Valley Road."

Dirk lifted a sheet of paper off the table to his left. "I don't recall seeing those names anywhere."

"Dirk."

"What?"

"Tinnerman Ridge and Long Valley Road. They're top of your list now. Evacuation imminent."

Dirk looked from one face to the next. "This is for real?"

"You know that item I've been holding in my bottom drawer?"

All color drained from the weatherman's face. "I . . . Yes."

"Do this, it never happened. Repeat the warnings during every on-air report from now until"—he glanced at Maya—"midnight. That should do it."

"Midnight works for me," Maya replied.

"Trumpet this evacuation report now to midnight, wind predicted to rise immediately, and that particular file gets lost in the process."

"Well, sure, I guess—"

Porter cut the connection and the weatherman vanished. "That went well."

Maya said, "I'm almost afraid to ask."

"Our pal likes to break all records for running up bar tabs at Castaways. Usually, he checks into the place across the street. Or at least, he does now. That is, after I watched him weave his way back to the car one night. I let him try and start home."

Maya shared the chief's smile. "How far did he get?"

"Ten, maybe fifteen feet. Far enough, as far as the law's concerned." Porter looked at Ethan. "How many homes are we talking about?"

Ethan was ready with the answer. "Four on the ridge, seven down Long Valley Road. All but two are absentee owners."

"Okay, I want you to go with Maya. She is setting you up on the observation post. That's as far as you get tonight. We clear?"

"Yes."

"Good. Ryan, liaise with the sheriff's department, then you're riding with me. They're waiting for your call." Porter rapped the table. "Let's get to work."

Ethan rode with the assistant fire chief and her number two, a sharp-featured young man named Raj. The last five or six miles made for very slow going, over ash-rimmed roads where Maya stopped regularly to speak with crew bosses. The radio emitted a constant stream of chatter, which Ethan did not understand. The voices barked, hoarse and sharp, but whatever they said left both Maya and Raj smiling.

Ryan texted four times during the journey. Letting him know the sheriff's department was in play. Asking him to pass updates along to Maya. Half-a-dozen words at most. None of the messages were so very important. But all were wonderful to receive. Linking them together. Even now.

It was fully dark when they pulled in behind the frontline tactical unit, a beast of a truck with two generators and an a/c unit drumming on the roof. When Maya pounded, a massive guy, whose fire-blackened features turned bone white around his eyes, opened the rear doors. Ethan thought he looked like a smoky raccoon. Maya stepped inside and shifted over to where a group of weary crew leaders stood by the front table, drinking coffee and studying a set of smudged maps. Maya refused their offer of a mug and demanded, "What's up?"

"We're good here. Fire front remains checked. New combustion is held behind our designated barriers."

"Where's the chief?"

"Asleep. Said to tell you, wake him when it's over." The man coughed. "He wasn't talking about the fire, now, was he."

She ignored the comment. "Everybody clear on their duties?" When they all nodded assent, she asked, "You've assigned crew to do the fake radio chatter, in case they're monitoring?"

"Roger that." Teeth flashed in all the grimy faces. "The four we can't ever get to shut up."

Another said, "They were born for tonight's action."

"Give them the go-ahead soon as we're done here," Maya said. "Both of our standard channels. They know to focus on the designated areas?"

"Tinnerman Ridge and Long Valley Road." Their grins grew wider still. "If the bad guys are listening, we're going to scare them out of their tiny minds."

"Remember, teams working with me, hold to the one designated channel, and stay as quiet as possible. If you've got something important to say, keep it terse and tight." She turned to where Raj had seated himself facing the side wall of equipment. "You ready to start?"

"Locked and loaded."

The crew boss pointed at Ethan. "This the guy bringing us to the dance?"

"I have no idea who you're talking about, since there's nobody else here."

"Whatever you say." He patted Ethan's shoulder as he passed. "We'll be waiting for your call."

When the doors slammed shut, Maya asked, "What's the word from Porter?"

"In position and standing by."

She pointed Ethan into a chair by the opposite wall. "Let's get started."

224

32

"Tonight's entertainment comes by way of my favorite dance partner." Raj glanced back to where Ethan sat against the opposite wall. Flashing a grin. Going back to his joystick and the myriad of screens. "This particular drone is a next-gen Autel EVO. Finest on the market."

Maya said, "He doesn't need to be hearing this, Raj."

"Sure he does."

"Because he isn't here. Remember?"

Raj snorted. "Save that for the troops, Maya. We're in my kingdom here. And the ruler of this kingdom says anybody who puts us on the hunt for bad guys is welcome to everything he can handle."

Maya crossed her arms. Sighed. Stayed silent.

Raj took that as his cue. "The EVO drone is equipped with a twelve-sensor omnidirectional obstacle-avoidance AI system, coupled with a dual-core processor. Two high-rez semi-twin cameras placed to either side of the drone's underbelly—a Zenmuse XT for thermals and the Z30 for optical and digital zoom, with a total magnification up to one hundred eighty times. An absolutely incredible two-hour flight time. The lady is whisper quiet. She'll slip in, steal your secrets, and you'll never know she's been within miles."

Maya said, "Do you even hear yourself?"

"Okay, we're coming up on Tinnerman Ridge."

"Hold it there." Maya leaned forward. "Where's Long Valley Road?"

"See the silver ribbon there? Okay, moving in."

"I told you to hold!"

"I'm increasing magnification, so chill, okay?" Raj grinned back at Ethan. "Amateurs."

"I'm trying hard to remember why you're not fired yet."

"Because you love me dearly. And because I'm the best." Raj glanced at Ethan. "Okay, Deputy Dog. Which house is the target?"

Ethan did not need to check his notes. "Number 277. Big stone gates."

Maya reached behind without taking her eyes off the central monitor and picked the top chart off the table. Maya studied the map, said, "You're too far north."

"Shifting."

The camera's position drew back, the moonlit vista slipped to their left, became stationary, and Raj said, "Should be on the money here."

Maya pointed to a smaller monitor showing the local news channel. "Our weather pal is coming on. Turn up the sound."

Raj did so, and they heard Dirk announce,

"We're expecting the blow any minute now. Strong enough to push the fire line through the current barriers and start an approach to Tinnerman Ridge and Long Valley Road. Residents are urged to evacuate. Do not, I repeat, do not tax the fire and rescue by waiting for the final order."

"Okay, that's enough." Maya glanced back long enough to offer Ethan a tight smile. Then to Raj, "Can you switch to thermal and check for activity?"

"Natch."

The crew's tactical unit was kept cold as a refrigerated truck, but the longer Ethan sat there, the less he cared. The thermal camera showed a wide-angle view of pewter imagery.

Raj said, "Okay, there are four . . . no, make that five people standing by the house's rear door."

"I don't see a thing."

"Little ants in the top left corner. Now they're walking away from the house."

"Can't you get tighter on them?" Maya asked.

"Not in thermal. Want me to move closer?"

"Some. A little. We're expressly forbidden from breaching the property's boundary."

"Roger that." The camera did a swoop and dive. "Okay, now there are six clustered by that big structure behind the main house, probably a barn."

"I see them." Maya leaned forward, frowning.

"Last time I checked, standing around talking is not a punishable offense."

Ethan asked, "Can I make a suggestion?"

Maya took a long time responding. "Go ahead."

"Say it's them. Say they're keeping the tow truck in that structure behind the house."

Raj shook his head. "If they haven't started the motor in the past few hours, it won't have a thermal image."

"Right. But if it's there, it seems to me they wouldn't drive it in and out through the main gate." Ethan watched both faces swing in his direction. "There would need to be a track or something . . ."

Raj said, "The man has a way with a point."

"Go to hi-rez," Maya said. "Scan the perimeter wall for a second access portal."

Ryan stood alone in the moonlight. Far overhead, clouds raced at rally speeds, their edges torn and shredded by the wind. But down where she stood, in the scrub and sorrel and mountain pines, there was hardly any breeze. A faint whisper of cold air drifted over her face and teased her hair. Ryan shivered, mostly from the prospect of having that same wind invade her world. Pushing the danger ever closer to her beloved town.

The radio clicked in her earpiece. "Ryan?"

"Here."

Porter kept his voice low, though no one else could hear him. "Maya, you there?"

"Roger."

"Okay, Ryan's by the back wall. Tell her what you just said."

"We see you, Ryan." The assistant fire chief whispered as well. Her words carried the soft electric tension of a feral beast on the hunt. "You're about two hundred meters from the estate wall. You need to shift closer. That's it. Okay, about fifteen meters away from where you're standing, you should find a track."

Ryan lowered her chin so it touched the mike attached to her collar. "You sure? I just scouted that area and I didn't notice anything."

"It's there."

"Hang on."

The going was easy enough, the terrain lit with a pewter glow from the nearly full moon.

Maya said, "Okay, you're on it."

"I don't . . ." Ryan turned in a slow circle, and there it was. "Wow."

"Talk to me," Porter said.

Moonlight illuminated two parallel tracks, little more than game trails. In the daylight, she would most likely have missed them entirely. The scrub had been flattened, a few larger trees uprooted and dragged away. All of this suddenly clear.

"Ryan."

"Okay. The tracks are too wide for a car."

"The wrecker," Porter said.

"Has to be."

Maya's voice remained whisper quiet, but tension lifted it an octave. More. "Follow it north. A hundred thirty meters, Raj says." A young man's voice murmured something that Ryan didn't need to hear. Maya went on, "The trail vanishes as it approaches the estate's rear wall. I'm hoping you might find something that confirms an entry point."

Ryan heard a branch crack. "I'm not alone."

"Yeah, Raj says a pair of coyotes are tracking your movements."

Porter said, "Ryan, maybe you should hold up and let me—"

"I'm good."

"Another ten, maybe fifteen meters, Ryan." Then Maya said, "Hold one. I show a heat signature on the wall's other side."

Ryan froze.

"Okay, they're gone." Thirty seconds later, "Raj says this is where the trail jinks toward the wall."

She had already seen it. What at first appeared to be six tall shrubs climbing the high stone wall were, in fact, attached to a stretch of fencing. Only the fence in this section did not appear to be part of the stone wall. Instead, the brush was lashed to a fifteen-foot section that could be shifted to one side. She stepped in closer, saw the wooden crossbars, and said, "Bingo."

33

It was approaching midnight by the time they were ready.

The wind grew in small stages. If Ryan and the others were not constantly watching, the change would have gone unnoticed. But it was real enough to whisper now through the surrounding trees, a constant rush of sound, urging them to hurry.

They needed two and a half hours to set their trap in place. The loads were heavy and bulky and stubborn. Soft oaths punctuated multiple bruised shins. Even so, they were all having a grand time, including Ryan, who stood by the fake stretch of fence, keeping watch. The firemen and deputies and Porter grinned hugely as they worked.

Twice during the prep stage, they were halted by someone patrolling inside the estate. Ryan cut a small section from the mock shrubs, just large enough for her to have a clear view of the unkempt rear lawn. The moon stayed out, and the guards were bored. They swept their lights in casual circles. They used the rear sweep as a chance to light cigarettes. Ryan and her crew had more than enough time to go quiet and wait.

The drone retreated for refueling as they were completing their preparations. Raj sent a second aloft and did a careful sweep of the entire region before zeroing in. Ryan's team shared flasks of tepid coffee and ate sandwiches. Ryan was hungry, but the sandwich smelled of kerosene and ash. She stuffed the sandwich in her pocket and went back to watching the rear garden.

Soon as Maya reported the drone was back in position, Porter joined Ryan and asked, "How we doing?"

"All quiet."

"Guards?"

She checked her watch. "Due back in another five minutes or so."

"Good thing they don't have dogs." Porter lifted his radio. "Sheriff, you ready?"

The older man was stationed on the highway west of the estate's main gates. "We're good. The road's blocked in both directions."

"Fire team leader?"

"I still say blowing a gas canister couldn't hurt."

"Negative on the canister." Porter clicked off his radio, told Ryan, "I always suspected those fire crews were pyros at heart." He took another look through Ryan's spy hole, then lifted his radio and said, "Okay, light 'em up."

Three minutes, nothing happened. Then the

first billowing cloud blew past. The smoke was so thick, Ryan and Porter both backed away, stifling coughs.

Twenty yards farther from the perimeter wall, they joined the fire crew. A line of fifteen waist-high barrels now stood parallel to the estate's rear wall. They were positioned so the gradually rising wind pushed their smoke directly over the residence. The barrels were filled with a potent mixture of dry brush and diesel fuel, with several inches of old ash piled on top. The smell was wretched, the smoke so thick the crew had to stand behind the barrels in order to breathe.

The barrels did not flame. The mix burned with a brooding orange glow, angry and acrid. The heat was enough to turn the barrels' upper lip a fierce red, illuminating a crew having the time of their lives. Ryan watched these burly guys grin and hum and occasionally dance in place with sheer unbridled joy. She turned back to the estate, thinking her ex would fit in perfectly.

Then Maya's voice came over the radio: "We have movement."

When Ethan leaned in close to the central monitor, neither Maya nor Raj objected. He took that as permission to roll his chair closer and take up position directly behind Raj's right shoulder.

Raj said, "Switching to thermal."

Maya demanded, "Can't you do both?"

"Not possible. Sorry."

"Why not?"

"System can't transmit two camera signals at once. Not to mention overloading the AI computer."

"Poor planning, you ask me."

"Roger that."

Ethan thought the conversation merely released a hint of the chamber's intensity. It was akin to a boiling pot with steam seeping from underneath the lid. He watched as brightly colored forms emerged from the estate's two main buildings. They sped to the second structure, where a trio of square blobs now glowed red.

Maya lifted her radio, spoke in the same tight mutter she used with Raj. "We have three engines idling inside the barn. Looks like the cockroaches are on the move."

The radios were hooked to the wall console's main speaker system, which meant he heard Ryan whisper back, "How many?"

"Seven people—"

Raj pointed to another pair emerging from the smaller structure.

Maya said, "Correction. Make that nine. Looks like two cars or light-body trucks and one mas–sive beast of a machine."

Raj pointed to the screen. "The bad guys are forming a conga line."

"Okay, they're apparently carrying loads to

their vehicles. All three motors are heating up."

Ryan responded with a soft calmness. "Sounds like we've flushed our quarry."

Porter said, "All teams, confirm you're ready, by the numbers."

"Team one, good to go." A litany of voices responded in turn. All were quiet, tight with repressed tension.

Standing by.

Ethan leaned back, taking stock. His chest felt banded by the same stress he heard in all these voices. His heart raced. He breathed in tight punches, taking in all the air his constricted lungs allowed, then releasing. He was glad for this chance to observe. Glad also he was not out there. On the front line. Doing what Ryan and her fellow officers treated as simply part of the job. He was safe here. Watching from a distance, removed from the operation and the risk and the enemy. Because that was what he saw. Enemy on the move. And Ryan and her teams were poised to spring the trap.

Suddenly he was flushed with a fear so powerful his body locked. He was the one responsible for setting this in motion. Here before him was his idea come to life. Which was great, in a way. But as he watched the thermal images move back and forth between the houses and the barns, while that small lone image stood poised by the rear wall, Ethan saw something else. The threat of having it all go wrong. The prospect of Ryan going down.

He was overwhelmed with a raw terror. Filled with the prospect of telling a little boy he had just lost his mother.

Raj said, "Looks like they're ready to roll."

"Raj, pull back to where we can observe both access points on thermal. Good, stop there." Maya keyed her radio. "All nine are in the barn. Okay, the vehicles are moving."

Porter said, "Ryan, back to your vehicle. On the double."

"Moving."

The drone's more distant position meant the thermal camera now showed the line of barrels, shining on the monitor like torches. Raj gestured at the movements on the monitor, and Maya said, "The two smaller vehicles are going for the main gates. The elephant in the room is headed out back."

Porter said, "The two smaller vehicles will probably split up when they get to the road. Teams one and two, prepare for the takedown."

The sheriff replied, "We're on it."

"Okay, they've reached the gate," Maya said. "And yes, they've headed in opposite directions. And the beast has stopped by the rear access point, two men are out and apparently shifting the fake fence, and here we go. Taking the left turn, heading right for you, Porter."

"Roger, their lights are visible."

Maya leaned back. Breathed in tight tandem to Ethan. "And . . . bingo."

Raj switched to the wide-angle camera, allowing them to observe as the trio sped straight toward the traps. "Well, hello, boys."

Porter yelled, *"Now!"*

The drone's camera showed three sets of headlights and flashing light bars come to life. They illuminated the night like silent explosions. Ethan winced at the sound of multiple voices. Sirens. Shouts identifying themselves as *police, sheriffs, get down, hands in the air, you're under arrest . . .* On and on, the noise went, until . . .

Ba-ba-baam!

Sharp cracks of gunfire. The three of them jerked as one. Raj said, "I hate this part."

Maya nodded. "That's why we're in here and they're out there."

Raj muttered, "Hate it, hate it, hate it."

Ethan found himself unable to breathe, much less nod agreement.

Porter came on, requesting, "Status!"

"We're good." Great gasping breaths, then: "Takedown complete."

"Injuries?"

"Nah, they're awful shots. Perps secured."

"Teams, report!"

One by one, the voices confirmed the teams were safe, the job done. Finally Ethan heard

Ryan respond. Voice holding to her normal iron-hard calmness. He forced himself to breathe once more.

Maya leaned back. "Good work, teams."

Raj said, "I love my job."

34

Maya and Raj drove Ethan back into town. Passing the boundary Santa, with his gleaming lights and tinsel wrap, had never been sweeter. Ethan rolled down his window and waved a cheery greeting. Another night working to save the town they loved. Neither Maya nor Raj seemed to find anything strange in the deputy saluting a street sign.

They arrived at the police station just as the last perps were photographed and fingerprinted and booked and jailed. The haul was massive—nine would-be thieves, including the former caretaker. The two pickups and wrecker were all packed to the gills with loot. Ethan helped transfer the recovered items into the conference room. Cataloguing could wait until after the holiday.

Ethan then stood on the sidelines, well removed from the real actors in this drama. He was glad to have witnessed what it meant to be a cop. Be a part of the holiday takedown. But this one experience was enough. Ethan had no interest in stepping further into Ryan's world. He watched her exchange high-fives with the sheriff's team, heard them share in-house jokes he didn't need to understand, and knew he had found his role in this relationship. He would be the bedrock that the wonderful silent boy needed. A man who was there in the good times and the bad. A friend.

Then it was over. Ryan walked him outside, said she needed to hang around and pretend to do paperwork. She hugged him, filling his senses with the danger scent of fire and ash and adrenaline and a long, hard night. One of many. He refused Maya's offer of a ride home, saying he'd prefer to walk. Waving a farewell, entering the night, knowing he would remember this hour for the rest of his days.

35

When his phone chimed, Ethan had no idea where he was, what time, or if his nightly dream had been granted time to take hold. He fumbled around, grabbed the phone, saw it was Ryan. "What time is it?"

"Almost two. I woke you, I know. I'm sorry."

He swung his feet to the floor. "What time did you get in?"

"No idea. Late." But she didn't sound the least bit sleepy. "Ethan . . ."

He rose to his feet. Fully awake without knowing why. "What is it?"

"There's a limo parked outside my door. The driver says she's here to make a pickup."

When Ethan entered their home, Ryan was preparing a fresh pot of coffee for the uniformed chauffeur. The driver was a heavyset woman in a standard two-piece dark suit. Ryan was nervous, flittering about the kitchen, constantly in motion. Trevor chose that moment to rise from his bowl, speed across the room, hover in midair, drink from the feeder, then pause long enough to give the newcomer a long look.

The driver watched the bird swing back across the living room and dive into his bowl. "Okay, that's new."

Liam sat by the tree, eyes big as a painted doll's. Watching and completely not understanding. Feeding off his mother's unnatural nerves. Too fascinated and curious to leave.

Ethan said, "Ryan, why don't you put the lady's coffee in a go-cup." To the driver, "Would you mind giving us a few moments?"

"Hey, no problem. I'm on the holiday clock." She accepted the cup, shifted her bulk off the stool. "Take all day, far as I'm concerned."

"We won't need that long." Ethan waited for the door to click shut, then walked over and seated himself on the carpet beside Liam. "Ryan, why don't you join us?"

"Do you want a coffee?"

"Maybe later." He waited until she slipped down onto the floor, close enough to drift a hand over his back. Smiling now. Excited. Nervous.

Happy.

Ethan told Liam, "This is an opportunity. I'm not even suggesting you should do it. It's totally your decision. But if you like, there's someone who would like to see your work."

Liam looked from one to the other. "Who?"

"His name is Noah Hearst. I've mentioned him before."

"The man in Hollywood."

"Right. The set designer working on the Elven Child project. I told him about your drawings."

Liam jerked with the sort of electric pulse that hit all his limbs at the same moment. Ethan feared the boy was about to flee. Shout his rage. Something. He hurried on, "I know I didn't have your permission. And he hasn't seen anything. But you showed me your work, and then we were out the door and rushing."

Liam settled. A little. "The fire."

"Right. Sort of. Anyway, Noah would like to see your drawings. But only if you want."

"The driver . . ."

"Noah is treating your work with the care it deserves. There's a risk of something going missing over the holidays, even with a courier. So he sent the limo to bring your sketchbook back down to Hollywood."

Liam looked from one to the other. His eyes were the only part of him that moved. If he breathed, Ethan could not tell.

Ryan said, "Honey, you don't have to do this if you don't want to."

Ethan said, "I can take photographs of your sketches with my phone, if you'd rather. But they'll be small images and won't show the . . . well, the full scope and power of what you've done."

Ryan said, "Ethan can just tell his friend no, and we'll send the driver away."

Ethan said, "Noah will take great care. And

he'll return the pages to you very soon. This is just a loan."

Trevor chose that moment to rise from the bowl, do a single quick swing around the three of them, then settle on Liam's finger. The boy stared at the tiny bird and softly declared, "This is the best Christmas ever."

36

Around noon the next day, Christmas Eve, they left the apartment and drove slowly around Miramar's main streets. They spoke in soft snatches, mostly staying silent, while enjoying the people and the crowds and the holiday decorations. Abruptly the distance between them became too great, and Liam crawled between the front seats and perched there in the middle, half in Ryan's lap and half on the central console. They stayed like that as they swung down the central avenue and found a space when another car pulled from the beachfront parking lot.

They walked, hand in hand, along the pedestrian lane, stepping aside for those coming the other way, never letting go of each other. When it came time for an embrace, it included the three of them. It was just that kind of day.

They stopped toward the far end, selecting a bench that overlooked the cliffs and the beach and the gulls. The sea rushed and rustled. The wind pushed from somewhere far inland, and the smell of ash and cold cinder was both distinct and unwelcome. Even so, the long-predicted desert blow had still not arrived. For this one soft hour, it was enough.

Liam had settled on Ryan's other side, molded in close with her arm around his shoulders. Abruptly he straightened and said, "I don't get it."

Ethan smiled at the china-blue sky and the gulls slicing their shadow script over the Pacific. "What's that?"

"The boy."

"Avariel."

"He might know elves now. But he's still just one boy. He can't save a whole kingdom by himself."

"He got others to help." Loving how he had been right to wait. Let Liam work through the book's events as if they were real. Which they were. On this day, it was as real as the feel of Ryan's body pressed against his own. "This old lady came almost every day to the park. Avariel trusted her enough to confess what his father wanted to do. She said the only way they could stop him was to find a unique animal, something that gave this forest inside the wall a special status. Something big enough to justify the courts stopping Avariel's father from stripping the land."

Liam's eyes went as round as they had been watching the driver. He shifted forward so he could look straight at Ethan.

He didn't need to say it. Ethan could see the realization there in his face. "That's right."

Ryan asked, "What?"

Liam whispered, "The bird."

"Hummingbirds had never been found that far north before. Originally, their natural habitats were all in Baja California. Down around Cabo San Lucas. Trevor's species was the first to be spotted. They appeared around the LA Basin in the early thirties, right when these stories were written." Ethan found himself mildly ashamed by how his eyes burned, recalling both the story and everything it had meant to him, back in those early dark times. "Some of the elves gave up their impossibly long lives, and became birds with the shortest of all lifespans."

Liam turned and watched the waves for a very long while, then asked, "Avariel's uncle?"

"Derion was happy to be one of the first volunteers. He was ready to join his sister. See what lay on the other side—"

"Stop," Ryan said. "Just stop."

And he did. Content to leave the rest of the story for another hour. When the waves and the gulls did not sing. When his heart was not quite so full.

37

They returned to the apartment. Ryan offered to make them cheese toast and coffee, and Ethan said that would be nice, but he then stretched out on the carpet by the tree, and in two breaths was gone. Ryan walked over and stared down at him, then went back to her bedroom and stripped away the pillows and duvet. She covered him, gently chided him to lift his head so she could fit a pillow underneath. Then she stretched out beside him. Three minutes later, she felt a smaller body nestle by her other side. Ryan passed into a dreamless slumber. Content. Complete.

She woke to the sense that Ethan was up and moving around. She drifted in and out of slumber as she smelled coffee and then sensed him kneeling beside her head. She opened her eyes and wished she knew words to describe his smile. How much it meant.

He said, "We're due at the restaurant in forty-five minutes." He looked down at the slumbering Liam. "Maybe I should call and cancel."

"Not on your life."

"But Liam . . ."

"He's wanted to go to Castaways for years."

She nudged her son. Liam groaned, but did not move. "He's awake. Believe you me."

"We can go another night."

"All it takes is the magic words." She lowered her mouth to his ear and whispered, "Breast of duck grilled over an open fire."

Liam opened his eyes.

Ryan said, "Dark chocolate cake with a gooey soft chocolate filling . . ."

Liam leapt up and scampered.

They showered in turns. Ethan dressed in the same clothes, blue button-down shirt and denim slacks. Ryan assured him he looked fine. Ethan asked her to dress nice enough that no one would notice his wrinkled state.

As they started to leave, Ryan decided, "One thing can't wait."

Ethan glanced at his watch. "If we're late, they'll give up our table."

"Ninety seconds. Less." She disappeared, and returned bearing two gifts. "For my men."

Liam did the true boy thing, grabbing the present and tearing away the gift wrap. His eyes went round for the third time that day. He slipped the sweatshirt over his head. The sleeves were six inches too long, the border fell to midthigh.

Ethan laughed out loud. "I hope you got me one too."

"Maybe next year, if you're very, very good." She handed him the present. "Merry Christmas."

He opened it, breathed softly. Closed his eyes. Opened them. Gave her a truly bottomless look. "Oh. Ryan."

She wished there was some way to freeze the moment. Instead, she looked from one face to the other. Taking it in as deep as was humanly possible. Then, "We better go."

Castaways was jammed. Even so, the crowd was in such a happy frame of mind, the tight constrictions around the tables, how the staff had to maneuver and bump the patrons as they passed, none of this mattered. The joy was all pervasive. Ethan was certain it wasn't just his own happiness. He wasn't just glimpsing the restaurant through a heart filled to overflowing.

Their table was right up next to the stage. Beyond the bay windows, a glorious sunset gradually faded. The clouds were massing in great muscular clumps, until the light formed a brilliant rim between the sea and the blank gray mass overhead. The light was so powerful it demanded attention. Even the waiters paused in their rush to look, savor, enjoy the moment. Then the sun descended below the Pacific, and the light diminished, and finally night took hold.

As if that was his cue, the evening's first per-former made his way through the crowd. Actually, it was four of them, and their appearance brought the entire crowd to their feet. Connor Larkin carried his young son and Sylvie followed, holding their twin daughter. She settled into a high-backed chair with velvet padding, as close to a throne as the place allowed. Marcela drew up a second chair and accepted the infant from Connor, who kissed his wife, waved to the crowd, seated himself behind the piano, adjusted the mike, and launched straight into a contemporary-jazz rendition of Bing Crosby's "Let's Start the New Year Right."

Liam ate and watched, his face impassive. Ethan could not tell whether he even enjoyed the music. So when the last bite of chocolate dessert was gone, and his plate was as clean as one boy and a spoon could make it, Ethan used the next break to lean over and say, "We can go if you like."

Liam turned from watching the trio of newly arrived musicians tune their instruments and studied him.

Ethan went on, "This kind of music is called swing. Connor and his friends give it a sort of modern twist. Some people consider what they're doing a type of fusion jazz. It's an acquired taste, and it's perfectly okay—"

Liam broke in with, "I wish I could draw them."

Ethan shared a smile with Ryan. "Say no more."

Ethan used the next break to thread his way through the restaurant. A busboy doing duty at the front station unlocked the door and ushered him outside. As Ethan crossed the street, he found himself joining a cluster of other pedestrians, all standing stock-still and staring into the western night. It took him a moment to realize what it was.

He tasted Pacific salt.

He walked to where his car was parked, popped the trunk, and pulled out his sketch pad and a packet of drawing pencils and pens. He carried them back inside, and waited by the hostess station while the group on the stage finished another Crosby hit, "Looks Like a Cold, Cold Winter." During the applause that followed, he made his way back to the front, gave Liam the pad, and said, "Go wild."

Connor and his group sang their way through another hour and a half. Then he stood and thanked them, hugged his wife and took the sleeping infant from Marcela. He wished everyone as perfect a Christmas as this one had already become for him and Sylvie.

Liam remained seated at the table, working hunched over the pad, while Ethan waited his turn to pay. Ryan stood with him, holding Ethan's arm with both her hands, leaning every now and then on his shoulder. Making it as fine a wait as Ethan had ever known.

As they finally approached the station, and Ethan thanked Marcela for finding them a table,

Liam walked up and announced, "I want them to have this."

"This" was a double image. The upper left section showed Connor at his piano, singing into the mike. Just his face, his hands, a trace of the keyboard. Connor's gaze rested on the page's opposite sketch, where Sylvie sat in the high-backed chair. Liam had drawn her holding both twins.

Marcela bent over the hostess station, craning to get a better look. "You did this? In here?"

Ryan now shared her son's wide-eyed expression. She looked at the page, at Ethan, at Liam. "But, honey . . . you never give away your art."

Liam handed Marcela the page. "I like the music. A lot."

Marcela said, "You just wait right here."

She pulled a passing waiter over to man the station, then rushed up the stairs, carrying the sketch.

It was after midnight when they could finally leave, ushered out the door by Connor and Sylvie and Marcela. Chatting in the excited and easy manner of people who had just realized they were becoming friends.

As they stepped onto the street, a great joyous shout greeted them. Cars stopped. People stepped into the street, calling and dancing. Clambering from their vehicles, turning their faces to the unseen ocean, laughing in disbelief.

Great clouds of Pacific mist billowed up Ocean Avenue, turning the Christmas lights soft as secret flames. Within seconds, everyone was drenched and chilled and delirious with joy.

Marcela and the solemn busboy and all the kitchen staff rushed out and joined the dancing throng. Sylvie and Connor stood on the sidewalk, holding the twins, laughing as Ethan lifted Liam and Ryan wrapped her arms around them both, a trio nearly delirious with joy.

They danced in place, laughing with upturned faces.

And then it began to rain.

Center Point Large Print
600 Brooks Road / PO Box 1
Thorndike, ME 04986-0001 USA

(207) 568-3717

US & Canada:
1 800 929-9108
www.centerpointlargeprint.com